CINNI WAS THE KIND OF MOTHER'S HELPER YOU JUST DON'T FIND ANYMORE

Cinni was sweet and sympathetic, listening to the intimate problems of her elders with a concern that clearly went beyond mere courtesy.

Cinni was sensitive, with a deep affection for fine art and elegant furnishings.

Cinni was magic with children, winning their complete trust and total obedience almost on sight.

Cinni was modest, clothing her already voluptuous young body in the most proper dresses.

Cinni was too good to be true—and too smart to be stopped. . . .

SUMMER GIRL

Great Reading from SIGNET

Summer Girl

A NOVEL OF SUSPENSE

by

Caroline Crane

A SIGNET BOOK

NEW AMERICAN LIBRARY

TIMES MIRROR

PUBLISHER'S NOTE

THIS NOVEL IS a work of fiction. Names, characters, places, and incidents are either the product of the author's imagination or are used fictitiously, and any resemblance to actual persons, living or dead, events, or locales is entirely coincidental.

To the memory of Jessie Louise and Roger

Summer
Girl

1

"CAN I GET you a taxi, miss?"

It was the elderly doorman, always solicitous of Dr. Tucker's pregnant patients. He stood inadvertently blocking the way as Mary Shelburne tried to leave the building.

Mary had not thought of taking a taxi, nor had she noticed the doorman until he materialized from some dark recess. She had been thinking only of the child that might never be born.

"Thank you, but I'm not really going anywhere."

She supposed she would eventually go somewhere, perhaps even home. But not yet. It was a rare luxury to be on her own, with nobody clinging to her hand, demanding a drink of water or a bathroom.

She left the cavernous Park Avenue lobby and walked out into warm April sunshine. A haze was in the air, a hint of summer to come. Miniature leaf shadows patterned the sidewalk. Flowering shrubs bloomed in the avenue's center mall. She slipped off her coat and carried it over her arm.

She loved the summer. Loved New York. Loved her life. This baby deserved a chance to enjoy it, too. Little Christopher, or little Daphne. She hoped it would be Christopher. Jason needed a brother. Jason was sensitive and shy. Sandwiched between two sisters, he might feel overwhelmed.

Three weeks ago she had almost lost little Christopher, or Daphne. This morning there had been another scare. Dr. Tucker had given her some pills and told her she had better take it easy. Get plenty of rest. Don't overdo.

God forbid, she certainly would not. All she needed was someone to clean the apartment for her, wash the clothes and the dishes, take Jason to the playground in the afternoon, pick up all the mess that got around every day, and settle the fights. And what about their summer at the beach?

Most important, who would pay for all that?

She paused at the corner of Eighty-sixth Street. Who indeed? Gavin? She hardly dared ask him. He thought two were enough. "A girl and a boy," he had said. "We've got it, the perfect American family. What more do we want?"

He had made that point, in fact, more than once. The first time was last year. Her third pregnancy. And then she had lost the baby. Gavin had mourned with her, but he had not seen any reason to try again. He didn't understand the incompleteness she felt.

Across the street, a westbound bus pulled away from the curb and wheezed toward Central Park. She should have been on it, going home to take things easy. But there were errands to do first, and even the errands would be marred unless she could get at least something settled with Gavin.

On Lexington Avenue, in front of a florist shop with outside shelves banked by potted azaleas, she found a row of telephones.

Gavin was "in conference." From her own years of office work, she knew that could mean almost anything. She told them it was important. They put through her call.

He asked if she was all right. When assured that she was, he reproached her for hauling him out of the "conference."

"I'm calling from a pay phone," she explained.

"Then you're not all right!"

Mary appreciated the alarm in his voice.

"Yes, I really am, but I don't know if I can stay that way." She reported what Dr. Tucker had told her.

He took a ragged breath. "You're talking, I suppose, about a full-time maid?"

"Good heavens, no. I was thinking of a housekeeper, maybe once a week for the heavy stuff. And then—"

And then the summer, when she would be the sole adult, and on call twenty-four hours a day. What if something happened? What if she hemorrhaged again and had to go to the hospital, or the children needed rescuing from drowning?

"And the summer," she faltered, "way out there, all by myself. Gavin, couldn't you take the summer off?"

"No, I can't. That's the whole reason we made this arrangement for the beach house. But you weren't supposed to get pregnant."

"Well, I *am* pregnant." She refrained from adding that she had not accomplished it alone. "Oh, well, I suppose if I go into premature labor at three in the morning, I can wake the kids and take them along in their pajamas. The hospital wouldn't turn me away just because I brought a couple of kids, would it?"

"Is that what the doctor said? That you might have premature labor?"

"It's not anything you can predict. That's the whole trouble." At the operator's suggestion, she dropped another coin into the phone.

Gavin was clearly defeated. "Okay, get whatever you need, if it will keep you happy."

"Happy!" she exploded. "This is your child's *life*."

"I didn't mean that, exactly. I—Look, this is a very important conference."

"Then you'd better go back to it. But I have to know, so I can start getting help before it's too late."

"You mean you're asking me?"

"What do you think I'm doing?"

"I thought you were telling me. Go ahead, then, hire a maid. A houseboy. A dancing girl. Anything."

"Thank you, Gavin."

She stood for a moment outside the phone booth, admiring the azaleas and breathing the spring air. Poor Gavin. She couldn't blame him for feeling trapped.

When the azaleas had revived her spirits, she crossed the street to Gimbels East and wandered among summer displays of hats, handbags, and bunches of artificial violets. She bought a pair of two-tone sunglasses, then rode the escalator to the children's department.

A swimsuit of aqua, blue, and lavender caught her eye. Beautiful sea colors, perfect for Fern, who had Gavin's green eyes and dark hair.

But Fern couldn't swim. It would have to be red, so Mary could see her even underwater. A horrid picture, but for once in her life she was being realistic. She bought a red suit for Fern and red plaid trunks for Jason.

An hour later, when he heard her key in the door, Jason ran to meet her. His arms were encased in gloves of gelatinous blue fingerpaint. Lucille Wilkin, the blond neighbor with whom Mary exchanged babysitting, set down the magazine she had been reading.

"Uh-oh, you caught us blue-handed. I was going to clean him up before you got home. How did it go?"

"Well—" Mary patted her still-flat abdomen. "It's okay for now. We'll just have to see. The doctor told me to take it easy. Get lots of rest. Gavin says I can hire a cleaning woman and somebody for the summer."

Lucille removed her bare feet from the cocktail table. "I suppose Gavin wouldn't be willing to pitch in?"

"He really works awfully hard at the office," Mary defended him. "And he won't even be there this summer, except on weekends. Do you realize I'll probably have to get a live-in person? I don't even know where to find one."

She sat down on the couch, suddenly tired. The thought of sharing her home with a stranger appalled her.

"It's a cream job for some teenager," said Lucille. "Lots of people hire teenagers for the summer, especially when they've got something like a beach to offer. Your only problem might be getting her to pay attention to the kids instead of the lifeguard."

"There's no lifeguard," Mary explained. "And where do I get hold of a teenager?"

"Are you kidding? They practically grow on trees. I'd apply for the job myself, if it weren't for Arthur and the kids. What about that girl who sits for you? Hilary?"

Mary considered Hilary, the bubbling beauty who played soccer with Fern and Jason right there in the apartment. So far they had broken only one drinking glass and no windows. Certainly, on a beach, there would be more room for soccer.

Lucille promised to ask around. "You just want somebody nice, who can swim, right?"

"Well, yes, that would help. And somebody who doesn't fall asleep too easily while the children are drowning. That's another thing I was afraid of. I sleep a lot when I'm pregnant." Mary kicked off her shoes. "You know, Lucille? I'm almost beginning to like this idea."

2

CYNTHIA RICKS WAS fourteen years old. A little young, Mary thought—the other applicants had all been fifteen or sixteen—but not so much younger that it made any appreciable difference. And she sounded capable over the phone.

Mary was tired of interviewing girls. Cynthia would be the fifth. She had asked Hilary first, but Hilary was going to Canada for part of the summer, although she had very kindly posted a notice on her school bulletin board.

As she had for all the others, Mary dressed herself carefully and tidied the apartment to make a good impression. She wore a black velveteen pantsuit with a white ruffled blouse. Her pale brown, almost colorless hair was combed into feathery waves. She looked fragile and ladylike, and no one would have guessed that she was pregnant.

She waited, holding open the door to her apartment, as the elevator hummed its way upward. It stopped, and for an instant, through the small round window, she glimpsed a pair of rimless glasses.

Then the door slid open and Mary formed her first opinion of Cynthia: dumpy and high-minded. The dumpiness was conveyed by a dirndl-skirted blue dress, a white cardigan, and flat-heeled shoes; the high-mindedness by something less definable. She seemed a cross between a nun and a nurse—the latter, perhaps, because the flat-heeled shoes were white. Her hair, a rather washed-out shade of blond, was long and straight. Her round, small-featured face had about as much distinction as a marshmallow.

The face dimpled into a pleasant smile. "Mrs. Shelburne? I'm Cynthia Ricks."

"It's nice to meet you, Cynthia. Please come in." Mary closed the door after them and led the way to the living room, where Cynthia was greeted with a blaze of afternoon sunshine.

"Oh, look, a river view! Isn't that gorgeous! The Palisades and everything. At our place, all we look out on is the street."

"Yes, we're very lucky," Mary agreed.

"It's a *big* apartment. And right on Riverside Park. It must be wonderful for the children."

Her voice, at the moment, was high-pitched and breathless, yet it still managed to sound oddly unexpressive. But her smile was very engaging.

"Quite wonderful," said Mary. "We have one of the best playgrounds, I think."

"And those nice cherry trees."

"Actually, they're crabapple."

"Yes, it's gorgeous." Cynthia took a seat on the sofa, facing the window.

"Please don't think I'm trying to pull anything, Mrs. Shelburne." She reached into her bookbag. "I just happened to be making these at home last night, and I brought some extra for the children. I mean, you know, I like kids."

She shrugged, embarrassed, probably realizing that her innocence might be in question as she produced a white paper bag filled with cookies.

Of course it seemed a little like bribery, but Mary was sure it had not been intended that way. The girl was much too sincere.

"Thank you, Cynthia, that's lovely. I'll get a plate, and I'll bring the children in so you can meet them."

"By the way, Mrs. Shelburne, you might as well call me Cinni. All my friends do."

"Cinni? Not Cindy?"

"Just Cinni."

Such a lovely girl, Mary thought on her way to the kitchen. Not especially lovely in looks, though. Gavin would be disappointed. He rather liked Hilary. But Cinni was the first one to think of the children. To put them ahead of the beach and the money.

Mary loaded a tray with her pewter coffee service and a plate for the cookies, and added a bottle of Seven-Up and one of Coke. She stopped in the doorway to Fern's room, where the children were playing Go Fish on the floor.

"Kids, come on out and meet a really nice girl. Her name is Cinni, and she brought something for you."

"If we can't have Hilary," Fern informed her without looking up from the cards, "then I don't want anybody."

"It has nothing to do with what you or I want, it's just the way things are. Come and see what she brought."

Cinni was standing in front of a glass display shelf in one corner of the living room. When Mary entered, she hurried over to help with the tray.

"You have so many beautiful things, Mrs. Shelburne. Do you travel a lot?"

"Not me," said Mary with a rueful laugh. "It's my mother-in-law and a few other people. I get about as far as the supermarket on Broadway. Cinni, do you drink coffee? I forgot to ask, and I really don't know what girls your age—"

"Coffee'd be fine," Cinni replied, eyeing rather scornfully the bottles of soft drink.

She was ladylike in her gestures, picking up her cup with perfect poise. And that dress—light blue, with short sleeves and a Peter Pan collar. Nobody wore dresses like that any more. Practically nobody wore dresses at all. It seemed, somehow, a mark of respect. For the job. For Mary.

The children came in reluctantly. Cinni held out the

plate of cookies and Fern daintily took one. Jason scooped up a handful.

"They're bigger than I thought they'd be," Cinni exclaimed. Meaning the children. "Fern, you're six years old, right?"

Fern nodded. "How'd you know?"

"Your mother told me over the phone. She said you were six and four. So Jason's four."

Fern nodded again.

Mary asked, "Do you have any brothers or sisters?"

Cinni shook her head. "Just a couple of fathers at different times. None right now."

"What does your mother do?"

"She's an interior decorator."

Mary looked from the children to Cinni, thinking they ought to talk to each other, but none of them seemed to find anything to say. She dismissed Fern and Jason, who replenished their supply of cookies and scuttled away down the hall.

Cinni said, "You have such a nice place here, Mrs. Shelburne. It's sort of like the place where I used to live. That was on the West Side, too. Does your apartment have a dumbwaiter?"

"No," said Mary. "Should it have?"

"I just wondered. Ours did. You know, for picking up the tenants' garbage and taking it to the basement. A friend of mine and I used to climb around in the shaft."

"Good God!"

Cinni giggled. "Don't worry, I don't do things like that any more. I guess I was about eight or nine."

"Wasn't it dangerous?"

"I guess so. Kids do such crazy things. But that's what you want a sitter for, isn't it?"

"Exactly. I can't be with them every minute." Mary explained about her pregnancy and the need to take it easy. She did not feel at all like taking it easy. She wanted to be with her children.

"What's the beach house like?" Cinni asked.

"To tell you the truth, we haven't even seen it. Some friends of my mother-in-law arranged it. It's way out near the tip of Long Island, and the house is nearly *on* the beach. I hope you're an alert sort of person. The children don't swim yet."

"I guess I'm pretty alert. I usually know what's going on." Absently, Cinni rubbed her hand along the side of her knee. "Your husband won't be there?"

"Only on weekends."

"Oh, he has to work? Where does he work?"

"With a plastics company. The Plastiware Corporation."

"A chemist or something? Or is he part of the management?"

"He's part of the management. A very minor part," Mary added, lest Cinni get unrealistic ideas about the family finances.

But she seemed almost too sophisticated for that. What other fourteen-year-old would speak in terms of business "management," or think through the fact that chemistry was much involved in the manufacture of plastics?

A very bright girl. Old for her age. And fond of children. What more could one ask?

They talked about Cinni, and about the job and what was expected of her—to keep the children from drowning—while Cinni's eyes roamed the room. She seemed to be taking it all in, the marble-topped cocktail table, the antique Italian chairs, the fake Oriental rug.

After a while she became aware of Mary watching her. Smiling self-consciously, she turned to stare at the painting that hung on the wall above her head. Her finger reached up to touch the surface as she contemplated the blue, human-headed bird creatures, the rainbow caterpillars under a small red sun.

"That's original, isn't it? Who painted it?"

Mary laughed. "Nobody you ever heard of. My mother-in-law did it. I'm afraid it doesn't really go with the room."

"It's not bad. The room's more traditional, but it's okay to mix traditional and modern, as long as it's mostly one or the other."

Cinni glanced again at the painting. "I like Van Gogh, do you? I like all the Impressionists, but he's my favorite. He sort of speaks to me."

Mary said, "My favorite is Botticelli."

The girl leaned forward and peered into her face with dawning wonder.

"You *look* like Botticelli. I mean his women. You really do."

"I wish I did. But thank you."

"You *do*, Mrs. Shelburne."

Cinni was flattering her, but it was nice to be flattered sometimes. Not only that, she was certainly a well-informed girl, with interests similar to Mary's. She could be a real friend. And that was important when they would be crammed together in the same household for two whole months.

"Will your mother be home this evening?" Mary asked. "I'll give her a call, so she and I can get acquainted."

Cinni looked surprised. "You don't have to do that." No doubt she felt adult enough to handle everything herself.

Mary, who understood very well, smiled gently. "I want to. And I should think she'd want to know what sort of people are abducting her daughter for the whole summer."

"You mean I got the job?"

"I'd like to have you, if you're sure it's what you want to do."

"Oh, it is. Thank you, Mrs. Shelburne."

The arrangements were made and Cinni went to say goodbye to the children.

"I'll see you in July," she told them. They stared at her glumly.

"Don't mind them," Mary said. "It's just that they're

used to someone else, and they looked forward to playing soccer with her, but they'll come around."

"That's okay, Mrs. Shelburne. I know they will. I'm pretty good with kids."

3
~

MRS. SHELBURNE WAITED with Cinni until the elevator came. Cinni would have preferred to wait alone, but she grinned amiably and waved goodbye as the elevator bore her away.

As soon as she was out of sight, she hugged and congratulated herself on getting the job. Fifty dollars a week plus room and board. Not bad. And the woman hadn't said anything about working papers or Social Security.

She walked out through the lobby, gliding over black and white tiles, past a wall of Pompeiian red with inset mirrors in big gold frames. Pretty nice, for an old building. And it had a doorman, too. She wouldn't have minded a setup like that.

The doorman ushered her out into a windy April evening. For a moment she stood looking over at Riverside Park, at the playground where Mrs. Shelburne took her children. Then she started up the hill toward Broadway.

She smiled, thinking of Mrs. Shelburne's reaction to her story about the dumbwaiter. She hadn't told the half of it. It was through that dumbwaiter shaft that she and her friend Marilla used to climb up to old Mrs. Binney's apartment, holding onto water pipes and gaining a shaky foothold on the rough bricks and crannies in the wall.

Mrs. Binney had been taken to the hospital following a stroke, so the apartment was empty for a while. The two girls went up to explore and found the place full of treasures, curios and pieces of jewelry squirreled away in trunks and cartons. They were things Mrs. Binney was not likely to miss right away if she were suddenly to get well and come home.

For two weeks they made those excursions, whenever they could do so undetected, until the day Marilla fell.

Well, not exactly *fell*.

It was her own fault, actually. It never would have happened, if she had only given Cinni that filagree necklace with the clear blue beads and the diamond teardrops. They had both found it at the same time, but Marilla got her hands on it first.

"It's mine," Cinni had told her. "You'd better let me have it."

She could hardly have made it plainer. There should not have been any problem.

But Marilla had to be stubborn. . . .

After she fell, the management discontinued its dumbwaiter service and plastered over the doors, so nobody else could get inside. But Cinni was safe, and her secret was safe. She had gotten Marilla's plastic bag of loot away from her, and she hid it in her bedroom before telling anyone Marilla had fallen. People had heard the scream, but they didn't know what it was. Nobody thought to look in the dumbwaiter shaft.

Stupid, stupid people. Cinni smiled again and watched her white shoes padding along the sidewalk.

It wasn't that she was so smart. It was just that other people were so stupid.

4

MARY CHANGED FROM her pantsuit into a comfortable muu-muu, one her mother-in-law had brought from Hawaii. It made her think of orchid fields and palm trees. She carried the coffee tray to the kitchen and pensively washed the dishes.

Her kitchen window, like those in the living room, looked out toward the river. This one faced north, and she could see all the way to the George Washington Bridge and beyond. She watched a tugboat struggling through the gray, choppy water, towing a pair of empty barges. *Trap Rock* would be painted in white on their ugly sides. She had seen such barges often from the river's edge.

The tug, the wind and the waves, made her ache with a kind of ecstasy. It recalled the John Masefield poem about a dirty British coaster in the mad March days.

The poem evoked a mood for her, a memory of something she could not name. It was only a feeling, that sourceless ecstasy, an atavistic affinity for all places and all times.

And it was all hers. It made her life exciting, as Gavin and the children made it satisfying. She could live in Delphi and Olympus, Venice and Venora, Luxor and Leptis Magna. To her, the iron fire escapes of New York

City were the iron grillwork balconies of New Orleans, and a potted mango tree in the dusty window of a barbership brought Puerto Rico that much closer.

She kept a postcard print of "Palm Tree, Nassau" taped to her kitchen wall. Down by the riverbank, there was a special place from which she could look north to the bridge and Hook Mountain. For some reason, it made her think of the Golden Horn, but that did not matter. She dreamed her own Caribbean shores and Constantinople, and she was happy.

With that contentment, she gazed out at the river and the bridge as she prepared the children's dinner, and watched the sky darken while they ate. As they munched their hamburgers, she recited poetry to them. The Masefield verses were still in her mind. She told them about the quinquireme from Nineveh, but they were not listening.

Fern screeched, "Jason took my roll!"

Jason clutched the roll until it disintegrated in his fist.

"He's a pig," said Fern self-righteously. Mary gave her another from the package.

Quinquireme from Nineveh. . . .

She had looked it up once in the back of the dictionary. *Nineveh, *anc. Assyria; ruins on Tigris riv. opp. Mosul, N. Iraq.*

The front door banged shut.

"Daddy!" shouted Jason.

Gavin came into the kitchen, unwilted after a day's work, his vested suit smelling of cigarette smoke from the office.

"Dreaming again?" He kissed her forehead.

Of course she was dreaming. She never stopped. Sometimes she thought she had dreamed up Gavin, who was dark and glowing and a far more vibrant than she.

"I found a girl," she told him. "You wouldn't believe my luck. She's quiet and polite and likes Impressionist art. And she really cares about the children."

"She'd damn well better," he said. "Good-looking?"

"Well . . . I did think of that, but after all, this girl is for the children, not for you."

"That sounds ominous. What is she, a fright?"

"No, just not very interesting-looking. But she's competent. Really mature for her age. Quite precocious. I'll enjoy having her around."

Fern said, "I want Hilary."

Gavin asked, "How much is this paragon going to cost?"

"Exactly what you specified, and I wish you'd stop trying to make me feel guilty."

"I'm not trying to make you feel guilty. I just wanted to know what it's costing." He took an ice-cube tray from the freezer, deftly twisted it, and dropped the cubes into a glass. He poured Johnny Walker over them with the meticulous care of an artist painting the *Mona Lisa*.

"You keep emphasizing money," she said. "That shouldn't be an issue, any more than the rent is. I'm sorry it's such a hardship. Would you like me to forget the whole thing, and go ahead and lose the baby?"

"Come on, Mary, that's not fair."

"What baby?" asked Fern.

Mary said, "I don't think it's fair to keep talking about money."

"Look, I'd like to be able to give you everything you need, gift-wrapped." He sounded rueful, as he always did when admitting the limits of his income. "It's just that—"

"What baby?" asked Fern.

"A very expensive luxury," Mary answered her wearily. "Gavin, I am sorry."

"What for?" His eyes rested tenderly on Fern and Jason. "It might be kind of fun, having another. I wonder what the kid will be like. It gives you a funny feeling to think it's already here. It already exists. We're not going to let anything happen to it, or to you."

He leaned back against the counter and sipped his

drink. Past his shoulder, she could see part of the bridge. It was a string of pale emeralds, twinkling in the late dusk. Close up, the lights were blue-white, but distance turned them green.

She sliced two bananas into dessert dishes and poured milk over them. It made the children think they were getting something special, instead of mere fresh fruit.

"However," Gavin went on, ruining what he had just said, "I can't help wondering if there isn't a psychological reason for all this. You might be trying to find some sort of identity through being a mother."

"That's not true! What a horrible thing to say."

He retreated apologetically. "I didn't mean there was anything wrong with it. And you're a darned good mother. But I'll bet you'd be good at a lot of things."

It had nothing to do with identity. She liked her life and wanted to go on living it just as she was, sharing it with her children and with Gavin.

She watched the bridge lights, coldly twinkling.

"Gavin, what kind of life do you want us to have?"

"What?"

"I mean, do you want us to be just two people growing older together, with—"

"I don't see how we can avoid it, Mary. Nobody grows *younger* together."

"You don't know what I mean."

"No, apparently not. Unless it's the 'together' part that you meant."

She did not know how to explain. He, of course, was happy with his life the way it was. And she was blissfully happy with hers, the way it was now, but it would not stay that way. Fern and Jason would grow up and away from her, and then she would lose it all—the picnics in the playground, the tugboats on the river, the Golden Horn. Only Christopher could keep it alive for her. And then Daphne. And then . . .

But poor Gavin. He felt so oppressed by the whole thing.

"No," she said, "it wasn't the 'together' part that I meant." She added, closing the subject, "I don't know what I meant." And stared past him to the bridge. Pale emeralds, glimmering.

5

EVERY DAY AT noon, Mary would meet Jason at his nursery school and they would take their lunch to the playground, where they would remain for the afternoon. At three, Fern would join them for an hour, and then they would go home, Mary to rest before cooking dinner, and the children to play quietly. Sometimes they watched television. Sometimes they fought and screamed.

The fighting made it the most strenuous part of her day. The playground, by contrast, was easy. She would sit on a bench under the trees and read, or talk with the other mothers.

The mornings were easy, too. She would wash the breakfast dishes, make the beds, prepare the lunch, and straighten the apartment. The straightening never ended. Things were always out of place. The heavy cleaning was done weekly by a woman named Sammy who had the energy of a hurricane and left Mary feeling worn.

The month of May passed uneventfully, and June differed only in that Jason's nursery school had closed for the summer. That meant that he was home now in the mornings. Fortunately he was a quiet, self-contained little boy, and could happily sit for an hour drawing pictures or working a puzzle.

Mary was glad when the month ended. The beach house, despite its inevitable gritty sand, could not possibly need as much attention as their Soot City apartment. Besides, Cinni would be there to help. It would be a marvelously restful summer, all leading up to that happy day in October when Christopher (or Daphne) would join the family.

On the first Saturday in July, they left for Matta-pogue. Cinni could not join them for the trip. She had telephoned the night before and said she had an emergency dentist appointment. She would take the train on Sunday. Perhaps it was just as well, Mary thought when they had shoehorned themselves into the overflowing station wagon. There would not have been room for her anyway.

Through sheer force of will, Gavin had them on the Long Island Expressway by nine o'clock in the morning. The traffic was thick, heading toward the beaches, but it kept moving. There were none of the expressway's famous tie-ups. They drove past tract houses, then fields, forests, and farms. In slightly more than two hours they reached Riverhead, and stopped at McDonald's for lunch.

After that they passed through the periphery of the Hamptons, and were in Mattapogue by one. The children were whining and hitting each other. "Is it much farther to the house?" Mary asked.

"Couple of miles, maybe," Gavin replied. "It's on the other side of town. First we pick up the key."

The town consisted mostly of a main street: a block or two lined with low brick stores, and impractical ones at that. Mary counted two antique shops, one expensive-looking boutique, one dog-grooming parlor, and—a ships' chandler?

"Do people really live here?" she asked, "or is this a movie set?"

"It's a movie set," said Gavin.

"Do you think they might have anything so mundane as a supermarket?"

"Well, over there's a service station. That's pretty mundane." He waved his arm toward the far end of the street as he pulled up in front of a miniature house with diamond windowpanes and a dark gold sign that said McFadden Realty. "I'll be back in a minute."

"Mommy, does that say 'ice cream'?" Fern was staring across the street.

"Yes, it does. Good for you, Fern."

"A whole restaurant, just for ice cream?"

"It's like Carvel. Or Baskin-Robbins."

"But this is a sit-down restaurant. Can we go there?"

"Yes. We'll make it a special occasion. How about my birthday?"

"Mommy, I can't *wait* for your birthday."

Gavin came bounding down the steps from the realty office, key in hand. He bounded because he wore sneakers. Sparkling white ones. Gavin's clothes never seemed to get dirty. (Why couldn't the children take after him?) He looked rather splendid, she thought, with his year-round tan, and the tennis shirt that matched his teeth.

"You'll be happy to know," he told her as he slid in behind the wheel, "that they do have a supermarket. Two, in fact, but one's sort of a deli. Probably expensive."

They continued along the Montauk Highway through forests of scrub pine. Suddenly, between themselves and the ocean, there was another village. Gavin slowed the car.

She saw that it was not really a village, in any commercial sense, but a colony of beach houses. A few anonymous unpaved lanes led into it from the highway. Gavin counted the lanes and turned at the fourth.

So this was where they would spend the summer. She had thought it would be a little more private, more remote. A lonely cottage among the rolling dunes.

These houses were set close together, although each managed to give the impression of separateness. They were thoroughly modern in style, with broad sundecks, picture windows, jutting studio roofs, or A-shaped roofs with eaves nearly touching the ground. Only a few had been painted. The first were left bare, their wood weathered to a silver-gray.

Noting the costly houses, the slim, sun-baked bodies, the meager but very haute couture clothing, Mary commented, "I'll bet they drink a lot."

Gavin was preoccupied with counting houses. "One, two . . . huh?"

"It all looks so smart. With a capital S. You know, the kind of people who swill martinis all day."

"I don't know anybody who swills martinis all day."

He probably did. It was exactly the kind of circle she assumed he moved in. Men and women both. And he loved it.

"It's like a little city," she said.

"A city?"

"Well—a community."

"That's exactly what it is. A community."

He stopped beside a white bungalow. It was smaller than most of the other houses, and was the second in from the beach in its row. Ahead of them lay the open ocean, blue and infinite. Fern and Jason screamed their pleasure.

"This must be it," said Gavin doubtfully.

Yes, it must be. It looked empty and deserted, waiting. It was an attractive house, nestled among rippling shore grasses and washed clean by warm wind and clear sunshine.

The house on the beach side of theirs was a sprawling split-level. On the inland side was one of weathered gray, with pink trim and a second-story sundeck.

The houses were unnumbered. Gavin knocked first, then tried the key. When the door swung open, Fern and Jason jumped from the car as though released by a spring.

Mary eased herself from the front seat, feeling stiff and bulky. She lifted her face and smelled the damp sea spray. Yards away from her, rollers crashed on the beach. Beyond the horizon were France, Portugal, the Canary Islands. She would be next to it for the whole summer, that timeless ocean. She would hear the surf at night.

The house, inside, was coolly dim, with plank flooring and unfinished knotty-pine walls. For damp days, there was a huge stone fireplace. Facing it was a conversation group: a cheap floral patterned sofa and two deep chairs, one that matched the sofa, the other dark green.

One corner of the living room had been designated a dining area, with a massive round oak table. Next to it, a door and a serving window both led into the kitchen.

"How about it?" asked Gavin. "Like it?"

She assured him that she did. He found it hard to believe. "It's not exactly your style," he said.

"What do you mean?"

"It doesn't have style is what I mean."

He was thinking of their home in New York, which she had furnished with hand-me-downs from their various parents. On her own she had added the mock Oriental rug and the marble-topped cocktail table, which he had not liked at first, calling it "cold." Now he thought it all tasteful. He was, in effect, apologizing to her for the present hodgepodge. She took his face between her hands and kissed him.

The children explored, running and squealing, their feet pounding on hollow wood floors. Mary checked the three bedrooms they had been promised before they knew about Cinni. Fern and Jason would have to double up so Cinni would have a room to herself. It would be expected. And what if Gavin's mother were to visit, as she had said she might?

For the next two hours they unpacked, made up the beds, shopped for groceries. Finally they were ready for the beach. It was midafternoon and the sun was at its hottest. They had brought an umbrella, which kept off some of the heat but not all of the ultraviolet rays.

They found the beach quite crowded on that Saturday afternoon. Probably the whole summer colony was there. As a private beach, it was kept immaculate by those who used it. Its fine white sand remained unpolluted except by nature's own debris. Jason managed to step on a crab shell and cut his foot. At least, Mary thought as she disinfected the wound, a crab shell seemed cleaner than a beer bottle.

By four-thirty, they had had enough. Too much, perhaps. Mary knew she was burned. Her skin felt stiff. And Jason, as fair as she, looked peeled and boiled.

They showered away the salt and covered their tender flesh with unwelcome clothes. Gavin was not really burned. He only glowed a little. There was practically never a situation that Gavin was not on top of. In skin tones, Fern took after him. She was not as raw as Mary or Jason.

Fern stood at the front door, surveying her new world. In the kitchen, Mary brushed a chuck steak with garlic butter and left it to marinate. She was planning the rest of dinner, when Fern shouted, "Mommy, there's some people coming."

A man and a woman had just turned in from the road and were parading single file up the path to the door. They were a pair of matching straw dolls, both small with paunchy bodies and spindly arms and legs. Both wore shorts: yellow for her, plaid for him. Each carried a tall glass sloshing with pale liquid.

The woman called, "Yoo hoo!"

Fern, without noticing that Mary had come up behind her, bellowed, "Mommy, there's people at the door!"

The man emitted a hee-haw of pleasure. "Get that, Claire? We're people!"

"Oh, nice," cooed the woman in a deep, creamy voice that had a slight rasp to it. She grinned through the screen. "Hi, there."

Mary opened the door. The face that greeted her was rubbery and shopworn, but thoroughly made up. The lipstick was bright, the eyelashes caked with mascara, and the hay-color hair was done up in a bobbing ponytail tied with a red ribbon.

"I'm Claire Fowler," the woman announced, "and this is my husband Ken. We're friends of your mother-in-law, if you're Mary, and don't say you're not, or we have the wrong house."

"Oh, yes," said Mary, remembering. "You're the people who found us this place."

Ken bounced on his toes. "People! She says we're people!"

He was a mousy man with a square face and a wide slit of a mouth. His hair, still dark, or perhaps dyed, was carefully combed and plastered across his bald spot.

They proceeded into the living room, carrying their glasses of Scotch. Claire stopped short and squinted at Mary's face. "Oh, my, tsk, tsk, you overdid it, darling."

"Yes, I certainly did."

"Your first day, too. Oh, tsk, tsk, tsk, tsk, tsk, why won't they learn?"

"It's nice of you to stop by," Mary said.

Fern asked in a loud whisper, "Are those Martina's friends?"

"Yes, honey, we're Martina's friends." Claire sat down on the floral patterned sofa and took a deep breath that expanded her in every direction. One arm went across the sofa back, the other over the side, while one thin, leathery leg occupied most of the seat.

"Martina's my grandmother," Fern explained. "She doesn't like to be called 'Grandmother.' It makes her feel old."

"But she's *not old*," Claire emphasized. "I'd swear she's not a day older than me."

Ken gave a malicious wheeze. "I wouldn't swear you're not a day older than *her*."

"Fern," said Mary, "why don't you go and tell Daddy we have guests?"

Daddy must have been aware of it. He walked into the room, crisp and handsome after his shower, his hair damp and combed in waves. The only trace of sunburn was a slight coppery hue. Mary introduced them all. "Gavin, these are your mother's friends, the people who found us the house."

"People!" crowed Ken. "We're people!"

Jason pattered out to the living room. Claire, gulping her whiskey, set down the glass and purred, "There's your little boy! Look at that, one of each, now that's what I call a family. And dumb ole us, we never had any."

Fern sat down on the arm of the sofa next to Claire. "Is it because you're too old?"

Mary said sharply, "Why don't you and Jason go outside and play?"

Fern slid down the sofa and started toward the kitchen door. "It's not the right size house," she informed Claire over her shoulder.

"No?" said Claire.

"Actually," Mary explained, "we have one more coming, but we didn't know—"

"Yeah, I can see, but not this summer—?"

"Oh, no, no, I don't mean that. I mean a girl. A sort of mother's helper."

"Now ain't that ritzy, a mother's helper. And what are *you* going to do all summer?"

Ken held up a finger. "Uh-uh. That's trou-ble. Two females under one roof."

Claire asked, "How old a girl?"

"Fourteen."

Ken was off again. "Oh-ho-ho, that's the worst kind. You gotta watch them teenie-weenies."

"Aw, Ken, will you cut it out?" Claire's voice had turned querulous. "If you can't find trouble, count on you to make it."

Mary said, "She's really only a child."

Ken shook his head. "Don't be too sure. Those ain't kids, those teenies in their bikinis. You gotta watch 'em."

"I guess Ken should know. He watches 'em all day." Claire exploded into raucous laughter.

Mary glanced at her watch. Must she ask them to stay for dinner? There was not enough steak.

A duet of angry screams burst through the window.

"Excuse me," she told the guests, "Fern and Jason are

killing each other." Grateful for the interruption, she hurried outside.

"Mommy, he won't give me my—"

"It's mine, I had it first!"

"Can't you two behave yourselves?" Mary confiscated the friction-powered police car. "You shouldn't play with this outdoors anyway. The sand will ruin it."

"Mommy, where does that path go?" Fern pointed to the lane that served the next row of houses.

"That's another road just like ours. It goes out to the main highway."

"Can we walk on it?"

"Of course you can, but not now. I don't want you going off alone, and I have guests."

"Please, Mommy? Just a tiny way?" Fern took her mother's hand and dragged her over a low dune toward the road.

"Fern, I *cannot* leave my guests."

"Daddy can talk to them."

Mary found her resistance low. She loved the explorations and good times she had with her children. She did not love the Fowlers. Martina, her mother-in-law, had met them on a cruise several years ago. Martina would take to anything as long as it talked, drank, and told jokes.

"Can we come here every summer?" Fern asked.

"I'm afraid not. It's too expensive."

"Then how come we're here this summer?"

"We're extending ourselves." And, although no one had told her, Mary suspected that Martina was helping to pay for it.

"There's nothing to see, only houses," Jason complained as they walked along the sandy road.

Fern gasped, "Oh, Mommy! Look!"

Tucked in a grassy corner where the lane met the highway was an old graveyard, its thin, nineteenth-century slabs standing peacefully within the boundary of a black iron railing.

"A cemetery!" Fern cried in ecstasy. "A whole cemetery, all mine."

"And mine," said Jason.

"No, mine, you dummy. I'm the one who likes cemeteries."

They wandered among the stones, with Fern chattering, Jason silent because the cemetery was not his, and Mary dreaming of a gothic death, of the sailors and whalers and their families who lay there. Even on that sunny day, she thought of rain, and black veils, of baby coffins lowered into the waiting earth, and mothers who believed in angels.

Then she remembered the Fowlers and was ashamed of herself.

"Fern, I think it's time—"

" 'Lost at Sea,' " Fern read, laboriously tracing the worn carving on a tilted, greenish stone. *October 21, 1832.*

She pounced on another. "Mommy, what's that say?"

"That's a name. Deborah. 'Cut down 'ere she bloom.' "

"What's it mean?"

"It means she died before she had a chance to live. She was seventeen years old."

"How do you know?"

"It says so. Fern, we really ought to get back. Daddy's going to be very annoyed."

"Can we come here again?"

"I don't want to," said Jason.

"Jason doesn't like cemeteries," Fern explained. "He likes *water.* You can get water anywhere, even in toilets."

"I don't like dead people," Jason insisted.

"They can't help it! You'll be dead yourself someday."

"No, I won't!"

"Stop it, both of you." Mary put a hand on each of their shoulders and marched them back down the road.

By the time they reached their house, the Fowlers had left and Daddy, as predicted, was very annoyed.

"What sort of way is that to treat people, just walking out on them like that?"

"I didn't walk out on them," Mary replied, stiffened by his manner. "I went to stop the children from fighting, and they hijacked me."

"Mary." His voice carried a warning note. "You just disappeared in the middle of guests. That's weird. Those people are going to think you're weird."

"Maybe I am. Chalk it up to an aberration that goes with pregnancy."

"You still don't walk out on people. They go to the trouble of paying us a friendly visit, and what do you do? You take the whole family and run off someplace."

"We went to a cemetery," Fern enlightened him.

"A *cemetery!* Right in the middle of guests?"

"Gavin, you have more than made your point. I'll write them a note of apology. I'll send flowers. I'll crawl on my knees to their house and kiss the doorstep, but would it be all right if we drop the subject for now? I'm getting a headache."

He stared after her, his face still full of little-boy indignation, as she turned and walked quickly to the bedroom.

She lay down, bolstered by two pillows. It was true about the headache. A nasty little pain had begun to form at the crown of her head. A Gavin-pain, caused by his treating her like a child instead of a wife.

He would reply, and perhaps with some justification, that she had behaved like a child, so what could she expect?

And yet there was a time when he would have understood. He might not have condoned it, but he would have known what made her do it, and respected her right to be, as he called it, weird. He would not have worried about what the Fowlers thought.

He had changed so much. Or had she?

No, it was Gavin. She remembered when they used to read Shakespeare together. Or spend their weekends on picture-taking expeditions, or exploring old houses, or bicycling to Staten Island. She remembered the time they sat up all night getting pie-eyed on Chianti while they listened to old French records, Edith Piaf and Charles Trenet, by candlelight, and shared their impossible dreams.

He would never do that now. It might spoil his image, even for himself. He would feel foolish.

He expected her to change with him, but she could not leave it all behind. And so she had to make a life of her own, and weave it around herself like a cocoon.

6

A BREEZE BLEW from the ocean, softly caressing Cinni's bare skin like warm fingers. She lay prone on her beach towel with Pete Mitchell beside her. They were surrounded by a swarm of legs and bodies, umbrellas and playpens and picnic coolers. Above them, a seagull hovered low in the air, waiting to pounce on dropped food.

She had never been to Jones Beach before. "Is it always like this?"

"You mean the crowds? Yeah, I guess so," Pete replied. "Oh weekends, anyway, especially now. July. Unless it rains."

His arm, all tanned and knotty, rested about four inches from her face. She could scarcely see around it. Pete pumped iron with maybe half the dedication of Arnold Schwarzenegger, and had, by her standards (and Pete's, too), a nearly perfect body. In fact, that just about defined Pete: a body.

Not that there was anything wrong with a body. Cinni was quite in favor of bodies—good ones. It just didn't make for a very interesting person, but since he was older, it might work. She wanted it to work. She had staked so much on it.

She reached out and ran her knuckles lightly over his waist.

"Stop being a kid," he said.

"Who's being a kid?" Stung, she withdrew her hand.

She rolled over onto her back and pretended he did not exist. A child ran past, sprinkling her with sand. The brat. She hated brats. From somewhere, she could smell cigar smoke. In all the great outdoors, you could smell one cigar twenty feet away. She hated that, too. It was like being shut in a coat closet with Mr. Hatter, who lived next door to her in the city.

It had actually happened once. He had pulled her into a coat closet when he was supposed to be paying her for babysitting. All the boats smelled of cigars and he did, too, and his wife was in the next room. Not that Cinni cared about that, except that Mr. Hatter was repulsive, and so she had struggled and screeched. In terror of his wife's finding out, he had let her go. Big, dumb coward. It still never occurred to him that he was repulsive. He tried to get a feel every time he passed her, and she could never ride the elevator if he was there.

You'd better watch it, Hatter. All you have to do is push a little too far. . . .

Pete said, "If you rent a locker here, you get to use the shower."

"So?"

"Well, they have men's showers and women's showers. I wonder if they'd let us go together." He laughed.

"Why would you want to do that?"

"Saves money. And after it, we could go someplace and park. . . ."

She rolled back to her stomach. "Why?" she asked, with an innocence they could both see through. "Are you going to let me drive the van?"

"Hell, we've been over that a million times. You're a kid. You can't drive."

"I *may* not drive, but I *can*. I know how."

He scowled, and she was pleased to see that he looked jealous and suspicious. "Who taught you?"

"Nobody. I learned from watching."

"You can't learn from watching. You gotta do it."

"Try me."

"I'll try you!" He landed on top of her and began tickling her. She doubled up, screaming.

"Damn you! You're a pig! I hate you."

He removed himself and she patted her bikini back into place, while looking around to see who had noticed. Probably they all had, but nobody cared. Pete chuckled softly.

She said, "You think you're God's gift to the world, don't you?"

"I am."

"That's what I said. You're disgusting. No wonder she divorced you."

"She didn't divorce me, I divorced her. And you know why."

"Because of me."

"Because of the baby."

"You knew the baby was like that since it was born, so why'd it take you a year and a half—"

"Because she let the baby *die*. She was passed out drunk."

"You can't really blame her for drinking," Cinni said.

She knew the whole story. She just liked to talk about it.

"It was my baby, too, and *I* didn't drink," Pete reminded her. "I stayed with her because of that kid. You know all that. I couldn't leave her to face it by herself."

"Yes, I know. You're such a big hero."

He flipped onto his side and glared at her. "How do I know it wasn't my fault the baby was like that?"

"It's not anybody's fault a baby gets born like that. You can't control it."

"I don't mean—"

She knew what he meant. She knew all about it. More than he did, even. She knew what had really happened to the baby.

It was a mongoloid. Retarded. Hopeless. Not only that, it had something wrong with its spine, so it would never be able to walk or even crawl, without a lot of operations. It was a horrible baby, but Cinni was not particularly bothered by things like that, and so she ended up being the only person they could get as a sitter on the rare occasions when they went out together.

That was how she had gotten to know Pete. And decided she wanted him. But Grace was in the way, and Pete would not leave her, because of the baby.

The only thing to do was remove the baby.

They never guessed. Grace had been alone in the apartment with her little son, and she was out cold. Cinni knew she would be. Cinni had been there earlier that afternoon when Grace came home, already drunk and carrying a parcel that looked very much as if it contained another bottle of liquor. Cinni had gone back to her own apartment, first snapping the lock on Grace's service door so it could be opened from the outside. Grace had obligingly followed her part in the script by drinking herself into a coma (with maybe a little help from a sleeping pill that accidentally got into her glass), and later the baby was found at the bottom of an air shaft.

Just like Marilla, Cinni thought. Both of 'em got shafted.

"How did the baby get to the window?" she asked.

"Who the hell knows?" Pete said morosely. "She probably put him there herself before she passed out."

"Possibly." She wanted to say more, but did not dare. She was proud of her cleverness. Too bad she always had to keep it to herself.

She did not even dare push again for marriage, not right after discussing the baby's death. It would have to wait. She was sick of waiting. Pete even wanted to wait until she was eighteen, so she wouldn't need her mother's consent.

"I'm not really so young," she said.

"Fourteen isn't young?"

"It's my face."

Her stupid round face. A baby-fat face. It was a little better since she had lost some weight, but it was going to look silly all of her life.

Grace didn't have a face like that. Grace had been

gaunt. (But maybe that was why Pete preferred Cinni.) And there was that Shelburne woman, stately and tall, with the fine cheekbones and the thin nose. It wasn't fair.

"Oh, hell," she said.

Pete turned to look at her. "What's wrong?"

"I hate my face."

"I don't hate your face. I like it."

It wasn't her face he liked, it was the rest of her. He just took the face along with it. She made damn sure there were compensations for her ugly, stupid face, and for being so young, and everything.

She pursed her lips and blew at him.

"Hey, cut that out, will you?" he said. "We're in public."

"What did I do?"

She watched him, waiting. She knew where she had him. She knew how to play him out, and keep playing him out, so that someday that body, and everything that went with it, would be hers.

7

THE MASTER BEDROOM was chastely furnished with twin beds. As Gavin said, it was just like a damn dormitory. He wondered what sort of people owned the house. Who'd want to live in a dormitory? Mary slept soundly and comfortably, until in the morning he crossed the narrow channel between their beds and woke her.

The light around the edges of the window shades was pale gray. "So early," she moaned.

"Quick, before the kids wake up." He lifted the sheet that covered her.

"Gavin, it's not even dawn."

"It is. We're facing west. Come on, this is our last time alone."

He was referring to the girl, Cinni. He considered her an invasion of privacy.

She sat up, trying to wake herself. He slipped the nightgown down over her shoulders.

"Awake now?" he asked, and kissed her neck. A tingle shot through her.

She held him closely, running her hand across his back. It was a hard male body, which she found an appealing contrast to a face that was vulnerable and boyish, with its flat, dark eyebrows and full mouth that could look either sensual or youthfully indignant.

"I love you, Gavin," she murmured.

A little boy. She wished she had a little boy that

37

looked just like him. But Jason took after her. Maybe Christopher. . . .

When it was over, he asked his usual question. "How was it?"

"Beautiful. Just beautiful."

"You're sure?"

She nodded. She was not a demonstrative person, and he never fully believed that he had aroused her. She wondered if he might have preferred a residue of long bleeding scratches on his back. But that seemed so brutal.

She noticed that the room was lighter now, although it was not yet seven o'clock. Could they go back to sleep maybe?

He lay with his arm around her. "I hear the kids," he said.

"Maybe we should have given them this room."

"It's not the light, it's their internal clocks."

"They sleep later in winter."

"I never noticed that they sleep late, ever."

He got up, and wrapping his cotton bathrobe around him, left the room. As soon as the door was opened, Mary heard Jason chirrup, "Mommy and Daddy are awake!"

Gavin turned on the shower. It was next to their room, and the sound of it roared through the wall. Above it, he sang tunelessly. It was supposed to be "La Vie en Rose." She smiled to herself. He still remembered those candlelit nights, and the Chianti, and Edith Piaf.

The baby kicked inside her. Yes, Christopher was part of it, too. Life was still done up in pink, although perhaps a different shade of pink. Or maybe it was multicolored. Hudson River gray, and tropical green, and fuzzy white with yellow teddy bears.

Later in the morning, Gavin and Fern went swimming. Mary straightened the house, with help from Jason. Beyond the windows on every side, bright sunshine glared on nearly white sand. The whole world seemed a blaze of clean, washed summer.

Next door, at the house with the pink trim, a woman in a bright pink caftan came down a flight of steps from the sundeck. She picked her way daintily across the sand and disappeared from sight. A moment later, the kitchen doorbell rang.

Mary went to answer it, self-consciously arranging her hair and smoothing her flowered tent dress. The Pink Lady had looked elegant and Mattapoguish, wearing that caftan in the morning.

The Pink Lady was dark-eyed and vivid, with a rose-and-cream complexion that harmonized with her gown. Her black hair fell in natural waves over her shoulders, giving her a girlish silhouette, although she was probably somewhere in her mid-thirties.

"Hi, I'm Esther Reardon, from next door. I just thought I'd come over and say hello."

"How nice of you. I hope you don't mind if I'm sort of a mess. We were just cleaning up."

"Maybe I came at a bad time?"

"Not at all." Mary invited her into the living room, served instant coffee, and called her Rose by mistake. The mistake was gently corrected.

"Oh, idiot me," said Mary, "I'm really sorry. It's all that pink, even on your house. I always associate names with colors. Esther is a white name, like a lily. Maybe because of Easter lilies."

"I see. Easter-Esther. That's interesting."

Mary learned that Esther had two sons who were too old for Mary's children and too young for Cinni, and a husband named Jack, who had his own advertising firm and took a month-long vacation in the summer.

"How marvelous," said Mary. "My husband doesn't get any vacation at all this summer. He'll get it in October when the kids have to be in school, so we can't really do anything then."

Except have his baby. Secretly she thought it was rather convenient that he would be home to look after Fern and Jason while she was in the hospital.

"You should have your own business," said Esther. "My husband's partner gets the whole summer off."

"How did he work that out?" Mary asked.

"He didn't. *She* did. She's me!"

They both had a good laugh, and then Esther said, "Tell me something. Do you name your babies by color?"

"By color? Oh, I see what you mean. No, by sound and association. But they all have colors. All names do."

"Like what?"

"Well, if this baby of mine is a boy, it will be Christopher. That's a yellow name. If it's a girl, Daphne. That's dark blue. It's really from the first letter, I guess. Letters all have colors. So that's why you have a white name, because E is white. Except that Ethel, for instance, is a little bit grayer than Esther."

"What color's your name?"

"Red," said Mary.

"And Jack? My husband?"

"Red, but a little pinker than Mary."

"This is all new to me. Are you an artist or something?"

"No." Mary looked down at her untalented hands. "Just a mother."

Esther stayed for nearly an hour. After she left, Mary hurried to finish the beds and change her clothes.

"Where are we going?" asked Jason.

"To meet Cinni. Remember Cinni?"

"I want Hilary!" he roared, in imitation of his sister.

"Hilary is a greenish-white name," she informed him.

They were about to leave for the station when Gavin and Fern appeared, dripping, cheerful, and tanned to a red-bronze.

Gavin seemed surprised at the sight of her, now in a yellow dress with Schiffli embroidery on the pockets. Yellow, probably because Cinni was a blazingly golden name.

"Where are you off to?"

"The station." She had thought he knew.

"Wait, I'll go with you."

"There's no time. You aren't even dressed."

"Just hang on a minute. The train will be late anyway. Trains are always late."

She waited, silently fuming, while first he and then Fern took their showers and put on clean clothes.

"Such fastidiousness," she muttered.

"You have to wash off the salt," Fern explained as they went out to the car, "or you get crackly crocodile skin. Daddy said so."

Daddy was right sometimes, but not about the train. It had come and gone, or else it never existed. There was not a sign of life at the station, which consisted mainly of a small brick building with boarded-up windows, a dusty, sunbaked track, and an open-faced shelter on the platform.

Then, from behind the shelter, emerged a figure in a light-blue dress, walking slowly with her head bowed.

Oh, Cinni. *Poor* Cinni. Mary hurried toward the dejected-looking creature, seeing herself at age fourteen, lonely, shy, afraid nobody would ever come, and then what would she do?

The head lifted, disclosing a smile. "Hi," said Cinni. Unshy. Unlonely. Unafraid.

Mary found some of the momentum taken out of her apology. "I'm awfully sorry. My husband and daughter went swimming and they lost track of the time."

"It's really okay, Mrs. Shelburne. How have you been? Hi, kids."

Fern and Jason stared coldly at this girl who dared not to be Hilary.

Gavin, at least, turned on his charm. Gripping Cinni's hand, he told her how good it was to meet her, and how was the trip?

"Freezing," she said. "They must have thought it was a meat locker, the way they air conditioned that train."

"And to think," Gavin reminded her, "you could have had a nice sweltering ride with us yesterday."

Cinni laughed appreciatively, and Gavin picked up her suitcases and started toward the car.

Mary followed them, trying to figure out what had changed about Cinni. She had lengthened—or something. It was not that she appeared taller, but only that the dumpiness had gone. Perhaps it was her clothes. The dress was the same color as the earlier one, but this dress was sleeveless, with a shirred top and a full, swinging skirt. She wore sandals with small heels, and her golden legs were bare.

Fern and Jason climbed into the back seat of the station wagon and tried to spread themselves out so there would be no more room. Cinni did not seem to notice as she slid in beside them, forcing them to squeeze together. Turning to Fern, she asked, "How's the house? Do you like it?"

"It's okay." Fern tried to look away, then turned back and peered closely at Cinni's face.

"Didn't you used to have glasses?"

"I still have glasses. Contact lenses." Cinni leaned toward her and fluttered her eyelashes. "You like? My boyfriend says it makes my eyes look big."

"I don't see anything."

"That's the whole idea."

"But where are the glasses?"

"Just like bits of plastic on my eyeball."

"*Yuck!*"

Mary turned around for another look at Cinni. A boyfriend? This child?

What she saw was not exactly a child.

She remembered Friday night, when Cinni had called about the dentist appointment. She had giggled when she said it. Nobody giggles at the prospect of a dentist appointment.

"There's my cemetery!" cried Fern, catching a glimpse of it through the scrub pines as they turned down their sandy lane.

"And my water!" yelped Jason.

Fern said, "That's not yours, it's everybody's ocean."

Cinni audibly caught her breath. "Oh, it *is* right on the beach, just like you told me, Mrs. Shelburne. This is perfect."

She scarcely looked at the house. As soon as Gavin stopped the car she was out of it, out of her shoes, and running toward the water, hand in hand with Fern.

Jason screeched, "I wanna go, too!"

"Later," said Mary. "This afternoon, darling. We're going to have lunch first."

It seemed as if it would work out after all. The ties with Hilary were finally broken. Cinni did have a way with children. Whether consciously or not, she knew how to win them.

8
⌘

FROM BEHIND THE blank façade of his dark-brown sunglasses, Gavin watched the girl scooping up wet sand to help Fern and Jason build their fortress. She sat with one knee bent, the toe pointing gracefully toward her other leg, which extended out to the side. She looked like a ballet dancer. The bikini that attempted to cover her was of some hot-pink shiny material that set off her tan, making it glow just a shade darker than honey.

He marveled at her figure, full and womanly, barely restrained by the ridiculous inadequacy of the bikini bra. It amazed him to see a fourteen-year-old with a shape like that. Fourteen-year-olds were children, weren't they? Still developing. Or were they? Perhaps he had forgotten. In some cultures, they were grown up. Without quite meaning to, he imagined himself reaching out to slide his fingers under the postage stamp of a bra.

"Yoo hoo! Gav-vy!"

Oh hell, he thought, as Claire Fowler hurried toward him on matchstick legs. She plunked down in the sand, all cosy and friendly, and rested a talon on his bare knee.

"How's it going, Gavvy? Everything okay?"

"Everything couldn't be better, Claire. I'd like you to meet Cinni Ricks. She's in charge of the kids this summer. Cinni, Claire Fowler. If it weren't for Claire, we wouldn't be here."

"Oh, well, I guess that's true," Claire admitted. "Nice

to meet you, Cindy. You've got a bunch of sweet people here."

"Cinni's sweet people herself," said Gavin.

Cinni smiled at him. He was a little shocked to see what a knowing smile it was. She couldn't possibly have guessed that he'd been watching her.

The talon slapped his knee. "What have you done with your wife?"

"I didn't do anything with her," he almost snapped. "She just decided to keep her sunburn out of the sun."

"Poor girl."

"I wish she'd come down, though, now that you're here. I think she owes you an apology for yesterday."

"An apology? Wha' for?"

"For the disappearing act."

"Oh, *that.* Oh, honey, don't you mind about that. I thought it was kinda cute the way she went off with the kids. She's a real good mother—as much as I know about mothering, which ain't much."

Cinni tilted her head, and her face dimpled in a smile. "Oh, she is. And so nice. I just love her."

Gradually the dimples faded and Cinni's eyes flickered over Claire. They were lovely eyes. He was glad he hadn't seen her with those rimless glasses Mary had described.

He wondered how much she really had changed since Mary first saw her, and how much of Mary's description had been wishfully inaccurate. Not that Cinni was even now a raving beauty, but there was something about her. . . .

"Gavvy, are you awake?"

"Excuse me, Claire?"

"I said bye-bye. Have yourself a good trip back to the city."

"Oh—yeah, thanks. Nice to see you, Claire. Regards to Ken." He watched with satisfaction as she toddled off to join a group of friends.

Cinni brushed back her hair, preening it with her fingertips. "She's sort of cute."

"I'm glad you think so," Gavin replied.

"Don't you?"

He shook his head. "Sometimes I wonder at my mother's choice of friends."

"Oh, well. Sometimes friends choose you."

The edge of a wave washed up over the beach, wetting Cinni's foot and knocking down part of the fortress. She squealed, then stood up and waded into the water.

"I just discovered something," she told him over her shoulder. "It's not bad at all. It was much colder yesterday."

Gavin said, "I thought you went to the dentist yesterday."

A sideways glance through her hair. "I did. Didn't you believe me?"

She took another step into the water and then another. He wondered when he had ever seen such a neat, round ass. There was something about a young body. It was crisp and unused, and yet luscious. And there, and not to be touched.

She turned again and smiled at him as she sank in up to her shoulders, then paddled backward a few strokes in a sitting position. She did not see the big one coming. It broke right over her head, knocking her down.

For a moment she was lost in boiling foam. Then her head rose, drenched. She managed one pitiful gasp before the undertow pulled her down again.

Gavin flung himself into the water. It was not deep, and he was stronger than she was against its force. He lifted her out of it, and supporting her in the circle of his arm, hurried her in to shore.

The children screamed "Daddy! Daddy!" He tried to reach for a towel to give her, but she clung to him so tightly that he could not bend over. She was two grapefruits pressed against his chest, choking and gasping for air. Jesus.

"Let me get you a towel," he grunted. He felt as though they had been like that for half an hour, but it was really only a few seconds. Maybe twenty seconds, or thirty. Too long, anyway.

She let him go and they reached for the towel together. She patted her face with it, then looked at him through wet lashes.

"Gavin, thank you, I could have drowned." Her voice was creaky and hoarse from the water in her throat.

"Aw," he said, deprecating his heroism, although she really might have drowned if he had not saved her.

She sat down on the sand, and he sat facing her.

"I was so scared," she confided. "It's awful when you can't get up and can't breathe."

"Yes, I guess it is."

Fern came and knelt beside her. "Were you drowning?"

"I must have been." Cinni huddled into her towel. "Usually I'm more careful," she added defensively.

Gavin agreed. "Of course you are." As though he had known her for years instead of hours. He hoped that at least she would be careful with Fern and Jason. And, yes, with herself. It would be awkward to have to tell her mother that they had lost her.

"Look," said Fern, "it ruined our fort. Can we make another one?"

Cinni nodded. "You start it. I'm still catching my breath.

Again she glanced obliquely at Gavin, then lowered her eyes and gazed pensively at the pool of water where the fortress had been. Absent-mindedly she stroked the outside of her thigh. Then her hand floated to the inner thigh, stroked it twice, and returned to the sand.

Had she been an older, more knowledgeable person, he might have taken that gesture as pretty much of an invitation. But at fourteen, how could she know what she was doing? It seemed quite unconscious.

He could still feel those two grapefruits heaving as she tried to catch her breath. Hell, he couldn't just sit there. With barely time to rip off his sunglasses, he belly-wopped into a fast approaching wave.

The water and the exercise had a subduing effect. He swam until she was out of sight and he faced an entirely different section of the beach. Then he started back.

Hell and damn, how was he going to get through the summer? It was maddening. It really made him angry. How could she not know what she was doing? Nobody could be that naive.

And then he thought: You bet your life she doesn't know. Only eight years older than Fern. Eight years was hardly anything. More likely the girl was copying some movie she had seen. Just the motions, not knowing what they meant.

When he got back to the children, Mary was there, telling them to come in to dinner. The kids were both excited, Fern screaming, "Mommy, Cinni almost drowned and Daddy saved her!"

Cinni bit her lip. Gavin put in quickly, "Nothing to get excited about. A wave knocked her down and she couldn't catch her footing, that's all."

Mary barely heard. She was too busy reminding him of the train he might miss. "There's only one more after that, and it would get you in terribly late." She picked up the pails and shovels, two sandy towels, the green plastic starfish mold and the yellow plastic turtle mold. "Come on, Fern and Jason. Daddy has to catch a train."

She was like a mother hen. He had not seen many hens in his lifetime, but that was exactly what she reminded him of, clucking and herding her chicks.

Not her fault, really, that there were more exotic things in life than what she had to do, or offer. This was her job. The only trouble was, she loved it. She didn't want anything else.

"You know?" he told her as they walked across the beach, past the white split-level house. "I think you'd make a great office manager."

She looked at him with a little frown between her wide gray eyes. "I don't know why you say that. I have no desire to be an office manager."

"Just thought I'd mention it. You never know."

He took a shower, dressed himself in clean clothes, and ate a supper of cold cuts and macaroni salad.

Cinni raved about the food. "You're such a good *cook*, Mrs. Shelburne."

Mary looked embarrassed. "Well, I did make the salad. I even boiled the macaroni. Thank you, Cinni."

At eight o'clock, Gavin and Mary went out to the car. To his surprise, they were followed by a flurry of, "I have to get my shoes," and "*Wait*, Jason's in the bathroom."

"What's this, a send-off committee?" he asked, pleased at the attention.

Mary was not so pleased. "Wouldn't you children rather stay here and play in the sand? That's something you can't do at home."

"It's all right, let 'em come," said Gavin. "They've got the whole summer to play in the sand."

He said it because Cinni was coming, too. She wore purple shorts and a sleeveless white blouse with one too many buttons undone. When she leaned over, which she did quite often to speak to Jason, he could see the lovely, round grapefruits.

It crossed his mind that he was being a dirty old man. But hell, he wasn't old, he was just entering his prime, and if the girl wanted to show off—

It really wasn't right, staring at a fourteen-year-old kid. Yet she *had* left the button undone. She was hardly the innocent he had thought earlier. He found it unsettling.

Mary had told him the kid had no father. Perhaps that was what she looked for, without quite realizing it.

How do you like that? he thought wryly as he parked by the station platform. Me, a father substitute.

Mary took his arm and tried to stroll away from the children. Poor dear, she wanted a little privacy, and it was not to be had. The children followed them. And Cinni, as she had been hired to do, followed the children.

Mary said, "It seems so bleak for you to be going back to work while the rest of us have a holiday."

"Well, that's life, isn't it?" he replied, forgetting for a moment how much he enjoyed his work, forgetting that a mother of young chldren never really had a holiday at all. He was being treated as a martyr, and he loved it. "Somebody has to pay for all this, and it doesn't come cheap."

"I really wouldn't have minded staying in the city," she added, stealing the spotlight from his martyrdom. "I love the city."

"It'll give you something to look forward to," he told her with unaccustomed sarcasm.

There was the train, thank God. On time, too. He kissed them all goodbye—except Cinni, the one he wanted most to kiss—and boarded as soon as it stopped. He found a seat, eased himself into it, and closed his eyes. He was tired and sunburned and, in most respects, glad to be getting away. It'd be a relief to have the apartment to himself, to do as he pleased, make as much mess as he cared to, and stay up as late as his heart desired, without a mother hen clucking.

He had not realized, when he married, how much freedom he was giving up. Little freedoms, to have peace and quiet when he wanted it, freedom from questioning and comments, from being judged or even noticed when he didn't want to be, as when he felt like watching late movies on a week night.

And worse yet, the freedom to dream. To have his life still ahead of him. To choose.

He opened his eyes as the train began to move. Fern and Jason were jumping up and down, waving goodbye. He waved back. Although he had looked forward to quiet and solitude, he would miss them. He watched until he couldn't see them any more. Then, with something like a pang, he sat back and closed his eyes again.

Into the darkness floated an image of Cinni in her pink bikini.

He banished it. Mustn't touch!

But he was not actually touching.

Mustn't even think like that. The girl was supposed to be under his protection.

Oh, well, a few lustful thoughts wouldn't hurt anybody. It was not as if he meant to act on them. Who was ever going to know his fantasies, or prosecute him for them?

He wouldn't even be thinking these things, if he didn't feel so stifled. It was all laid out for him. No room to move. He remembered the good old days, when at three o'clock in the morning they might be having coffee somewhere in Greenwich Village because the next day was Sunday and they could sleep late. Or when they would sit around getting bombed on cheap wine while they listened to some old recording by Edith Piaf, which made Mary think Montmartre, where neither of them had ever been, and made him think of Mary. Or those evenings when they would go up to the roof and take slow-speed photographs of the night.

Was it the kids? Was that what had taken it all away? No matter what nostalgia he felt, it always came back to Mary, so it couldn't be Mary *per se* that stifled him now. And yet in a way it was. She had created the life that trapped them both. That was what he liked about his afternoon of Cinni-watching. He had been young again—really young, not an ancient twenty-nine. Young and free and unobligated.

With his life still ahead of him.

That was it. It made a hell of a lot of difference if you knew your choices were yet to be made, and you could do anything you wanted with your life.

A hell of a lot of difference.

9

MARY WOKE THE next morning and lay in bed wondering what had happened to the children. It was already seven-thirty and they had not waked her, either deliberately or with their usual noise. She listened, and from far off, heard the clink of dishes. She opened the bedroom door and looked down the hall. There they were, the three of them, Fern, Jason, and Cinni, all seated around the kitchen table like a happy family.

Relieved, she closed the door and went back to bed, but did not sleep. Her thoughts floated like summer clouds. She basked in the luxury of having Cinni to take over her responsibilities. It was a long time since she had been able to float like this.

The noise crescendoed as they came back to their rooms to get dressed, and then she began to hear the slamming of screen doors. Fern and Jason were heady with the freedom to go in and out as they pleased, without waiting for someone to escort them, without even waiting for an elevator.

By eight o'clock, she could no longer rest. The doors were too much. She got up, took a shower and dressed, and was standing in the bedroom combing her hair when Cinni materialized in the mirror before her.

"You startled me," Mary said, turning around.

Cinni smiled. "I didn't mean to. I was just wondering, Mrs. Shelburne, did you ever think of coloring it?"

"My hair, you mean?"

"Yes, don't you think so? It would look really nice if you got it styled, had a good cut, and put some color in it. You don't look old enough—I mean, I know it's none of my business, but I don't think any woman under eighty should let her hair go gray. I think you owe it to yourself to keep it nice."

"Gray?" Mary began to understand. "Oh, it isn't really gray. It's always been this color, even when I was a child."

Cinni's lips parted in distress, perhaps embarrassment.

"Oh—well—it *is* an interesting color. A very ashy brown. Really—ashes. I never saw hair that shade. But I'm afraid a lot of people are going to think it's gray."

"I daresay a lot of people do," said Mary.

"Well . . . it's your hair, I guess."

"Yes, it does seem to be. But I'll think about what you've said." She did not want the girl to feel snubbed. It had been sweet of her to care.

Although nobody had ever before mistaken Mary's hair for gray.

Cinni backed away a few steps and then circled around to the other side of Mary. She put her thumb against her teeth and bit on the nail.

"I'm really being awful, I know, but as long as we're on the subject, I've been wondering why you don't use more eye makeup."

"I don't use any."

"Yes, I can see that. But it would really give them color. Make them alive. You could try some green shadow, or violet, and some liner, and maybe mascara for evenings. They're not bad, you know. They just need a little color and emphasis."

She really was being rather overbearing. It began to get under Mary's skin.

"You seem to be quite an expert. Which surprises me, since you don't wear much make-up yourself."

The smile again, all dimples. "Oh, you know how girls fool around with cosmetics. You pick up quite a lot."

It did not seem to occur to her that Mary, too, had once been a girl, and had probably fooled around with cosmetics.

"Well, thank you for passing it on," said Mary.

"It's nothing, really. I hope I didn't hurt your feelings, or anything. I just thought it was a shame, when you've got basically good equipment. You know, being tall and lanky, you could even be a model. Or I mean you *could* have been. You'd have to start much younger."

"Yes, I suppose you would. Fortunately it's something that never appealed to me."

Her hair was combed. Long since combed. She had only been fussing nervously. But why nervously? Well, why not, being dissected by a fourteen-year-old?

"Do you want me to take the kids to the beach, Mrs. Shelburne?"

"Maybe later. It's still early, isn't it? In an hour or so we can all go."

"Oh, that's okay. You're supposed to be resting. I don't mind going alone with them, and the earlier, the better, before the sun gets too bright. I'll see that they get ready."

She was gone before Mary could say anything further. Mary sat down on her unmade bed, feeling as though a light had gone out somewhere. She could not quite place the source of the feeling. It might have had something to do with Cinni, but it was ridiculous to be depressed over the possibily untactful prattlings of a young teenager.

She *had* wanted to go to the beach. What else was there to do? But Cinni's whole purpose was to mind the children so Mary could rest, and naturally Cinni wanted to prove her worth.

Mary slipped off her shoes and lay back on the bed. Now she was resting, the way she was "supposed" to.

In all fairness, she couldn't blame the girl for saying even that. Probably Gavin had given her a lecture, and she was only being conscientious about her duties. Mary closed her eyes and was almost asleep when they came into her room to announce that they were off.

Cinni wore a white bikini with pink coin dots. It looked like a funny little diaper. Her skin was golden and smooth. Mary had never tanned like that. She only burned and then faded back to her original color.

"Remember, Cinni's in charge," she told the children. "Do exactly what she says. And, Cinni, please be careful that Jason doesn't get more burned. Take the beach umbrella, and make him wear a shirt when he's not in the water."

The children seemed happy and excited. She got up and watched through a window as they left. Then she straightened her bed, ate a light breakfast, and wondered what to do with herself.

She stood outside the kitchen door. The clear air and the sea breeze were so very different from the playground at Ninety-seventh Street, where she would be at this hour if they were not in Mattapogue.

Yet she loved the playground and the mornings there with her children. She loved the muggy air, the trees, the sandboxes and the sprinkler. She felt a longing for both places at once. It reminded her of something she could not quite name. A juxtaposition of the place where her own children played, and something from her childhood—perhaps only a picture of white laundry flapping in brilliant sunshine, and seagulls above, wheeling under puffs of clouds.

She remembered the graveyard and started walking up the road. What had it been like back then, when Deborah lived and died? Deborah could scarcely have imagined all these pleasure-seeking summer people building fancy houses just so they could spend their days lolling on the beach, and their evenings visiting back and forth with tinkling glasses of whiskey.

The walk was hot and up a slight incline, but it did not take long. She stood at the edge of the graveyard, unconscious of the cars passing along the highway just beyond it. There were no cars. Time, to her, had turned backward. She imagined how it was when the graves were new, and whaling men sailed out of Mattapogue harbor in their tall-masted ships.

She stepped over the iron rail, and high grasses swished around her legs. How peaceful it was. Not even cared for. There were no cut flowers or mowed lawns. These people could sleep forever.

She walked about with her hands in the pockets of her denim dress. Her fingers discovered a tiny shell Jason had given her on Saturday. It was chipped, but still delicate, with a pearly amber iridescence. She placed it carefully just below the headstone of Deborah, who had died 'ere she bloomed.

It made her think of a poem. She tried to remember the words. They were gone.

Never mind. She knew where to find them. It was A. E. Housman. Something about bringing to a grave "No spray that ever buds in spring."

She shivered with winter thoughts and felt the hot sun on her shoulders, the suffocating air in her lungs. When she closed her eyes, she saw the graveyard in black and white, stark against the wild grasses—and, if she were to shoot from below, the sky.

"Oh, why didn't I think of it?" she exclaimed aloud. She hesitated for only a moment—it was a nuisance to go all the way back—and then she started down the road to get her camera.

She was not exactly resting. She was too excited to rest. Memories tumbled over each other of the beautiful effects she and Gavin used to achieve when they had their bathroom fixed as a darkroom, of the cartons at home filled with stunning eight-by-tens, arty shots of girders, monuments, clouds, and faces. She had not even used her good Yashica in several years, but had snapped pictures of the children with an Instamatic. Children did not want to stand still while she adjusted f stops for artistry. She loaded the Yashica with film and took along its instruction book to help with all she had forgotten.

Returning to the graveyard, she felt a little guilty that

Fern was not with her. Fern had so enjoyed their expedition on Saturday.

But she enjoyed the beach, too, and it was good for her, and the cemetery would be there all summer. And, dammit, a mother needed some life of her own.

She paused to consider that last idea. The thought, although not a new one for womankind, was new to her. It almost amounted to heresy. But after the shock wore off, she found it a rather pleasant concept.

She would take a picture of Deborah's stone first, because she found it so moving. She stood as close as she could, and angled the shot, hoping to catch a gleam from the iridescent shell she had placed there. She imagined the picture in an album with the A. E. Housman poem as a caption.

Perhaps even a book. If the photographs were good enough, maybe someday an art book . . .

Ridiculous. She had no talent. It was only for fun. But she liked to think she was doing it for some more serious reason.

She took twelve more shots of the graveyard, then crossed the road to a swampy area where she had noticed a grove of small trees with bare white branches that grew in odd, twisted shapes. Skeletal trees. She would find a poem for that, too.

And when she got back to the city, she would set up her darkroom again.

She returned to the house and entered by the kitchen door. She found the children seated at the table, waiting patiently while Cinni spread sandwiches with peanut butter and jelly and neatly quartered them.

"Oh, hi, Mrs. Shelburne," Cinni said, adding unnecessarily, "We were about to have lunch."

Fern asked, "Where did you go, Mommy?"

"Out. To take some pictures."

Cinni said, "Oh, you're into photography. I did that, too, for a while. It's fun, isn't it?"

"A barrel of laughs," replied Mary, and went to her room to put away the camera. She removed the film, threaded in another, and cleaned the lens with a soft brush. And wondered why she should feel so put down by Cinni's innocent remark. The girl only meant to be friendly. If she seemed a bit gauche at times—well, she was really very young.

She returned to the kitchen to hear Cinni telling the children, "Now you eat up, and then we'll have a little rest, and maybe about three o'clock we can go back."

Mary said, "Not back to the beach, I hope."

Three faces turned to look at her. Fern asked, "Why not?"

"Because Jason won't have any skin left, that's why. Look at his face and arms."

Cinni regarded Jason, who was munching on his sandwich, then lifted one shoulder in an almost imperceptible shrug. "Yes, he did get a little burned. That's why we're waiting till three. The sun won't be so strong then."

She spoke with great authority. *What* authority? Since when—?

"Cinni, I honestly think Jason had better stay inside this afternoon."

Jason let out a roar. "I wanna go to the beach."

Cinni reached out, placing her fingers gently on Mary's arm. "It's okay, Mrs. Shelburne, Jason's going to be more careful this afternoon. Aren't you, Jason? He came out from under the umbrella this morning because he was playing and forgot, but he won't do that again, will you, precious?"

Solemnly Jason shook his head, holding Cinni's eyes. Promising *her*.

Mary felt a sudden, irrational anger, which she promptly quelled. It would not do to start arguing with them. She would only sound childish. Resentful.

"Well, it's against my better judgment," she said. "It isn't only a matter of umbrella, you know. It's all the glare from the sand and water."

She realized immediately that if she gave in this time,

they would have bested her, and it would be even easier for them to do it next time.

Yet to turn right around and contradict herself would be equally weak. She let it pass.

"But only this once," she added. "If people are going to be foolhardy about their sunburns, we'll have to make stricter rules."

"Right, Mrs. Shelburne." Cinni agreed completely. And when she went to the beach that afternoon, she carried the umbrella and a heavy shirt for Jason. Mary stood at the screen door, watching them go. Watching Cinni lead the procession, holding the umbrella like a banner. Mary would check later to be sure they were obeying her rules.

She was so intent upon watching the banner lose itself in the beach population that she did not see Claire Fowler until a rasping "Yoo hoo!" pierced her ear.

Claire was scurrying across the road, a spindly-legged figure in flaring yellow shorts and Dr. Scholl's Exercise Sandals.

"Oh, hello, Claire."

Mary had not seen her since Saturday, and wondered if she ought to apologize for walking out on her.

Claire's sandals clattered into the living room. "Well, well, well, that's some dish you got there."

"Dish?"

"The *au pair*." Claire jerked her head toward the beach.

"Oh. Cinni. Her name's Cinni. Claire, it's nice to see you. Please sit down." Mary led the way to the sofa. "Listen, I'm sorry about the other day. I didn't mean to go off like that, but—"

"Aw, it's okay. The kids got their rights, too. We were gonna leave anyway, we had this party. Well, well." Claire's head swiveled and darted as she looked around the room. "So Gavvy's gone and you're all alone."

She made it sound as if they had gotten divorced.

"I'm hardly alone," Mary pointed out. "We're fairly teeming with people here. Cinni's marvelous with the children, and they're having such a good time. It's just the way I think family life should be."

"Yeah?" Claire was left blinking. "How do you mean? Without Gavvy?"

"No, no. Just having the children around. Keeping them with me. You see, when I was growing up, my parents used to ship me off to camp every summer whether I liked it or not, just so they could go on nice trips together. I always swore I'd never do that to my own children. I believe in being together."

Claire understood. "You felt kinda like they were sweeping you under a rug."

"I think they meant well. In their own way, they probably figured it was good for me."

From the vantage point of nearly thirty years, she could see that now. But she wondered if maybe, at the time, she hadn't felt kinda like they *were* sweeping her under a rug.

"Claire, would you like some coffee? Iced tea? Beer? I'm sorry, that's all we have."

Claire chose beer. When the glass was in her hand, she took a long drink, then a long breath, and was ready to disclose what she had come for.

"Look, honey, I don't want to make trouble for you or anything like that, but honestly, it's my frank opinion that you oughta get rid of that girl, and the sooner the better."

"Who, Cinni? Whatever for? She's a wonderful girl."

Claire leaned toward her and spoke in confidential tones. "I'll tell you what for, and don't get mad at me, it's for your own good. The reason is, honey, it ain't safe, as the saying goes. I was down on the beach yesterday, and I saw them."

"Yesterday? But—Gavin was there." (Had Cinni fallen asleep? Neglected them in some way?)

"And that, honey, is exactly what I mean. Gavvy was

there—that's how I met the kid, Gavvy introduced us—and she was all decked out in this little bikini—"

Mary said, "That's what they all wear. All young girls wear bikinis."

"—and he couldn't take his eyes off her. He was wearing those dark glasses, but *I* could tell. And she was playing up to him like you never saw."

"Playing up to him? But, Clare, she's only fourteen. She's a child."

"I'm telling you what it looked like to me. And believe me, honey, I wasn't born yesterday."

Mary could believe it. About Claire not being born yesterday.

She pondered the other for a moment. Cinni and Gavin. It was all so preposterous. Obviously Claire had a dirty mind. That was all there was to it.

Feeling called upon to say something, she remarked, "I guess a girl that age likes to be reassured that she's attractive."

"She's no worse off than most," said Claire. "But whatever, I thought you oughta know, because you're a very nice person and I'd hate for anything to happen."

"I don't think anything will happen. They're both too responsible, really. I suppose you can't stop a man from admiring an attractive girl. It's like—well, the way you'd admire a painting. Or a sunset."

"The way I see it, there's no point in *askin'* for trouble. After all, it's kind of a dynamite situation, having a girl like that in the same house with a young man."

The conversation, the very premise of it, began to irritate Mary.

"Gavin won't be around much, you know. If he were going to be, I wouldn't need Cinni." She spread her hands. "As you can see, I'm rather pregnant. I've been having some trouble with it, and the doctor told me to take it easy. I just need someone here to share the load."

"Yeah, I understand." Uncertainty dripped from Claire's voice. "But I thought you oughta know." She leaned back, closed her eyes, and drained her glass.

Mary glanced down at her own enlarged belly under the denim dress. Where was the madonna mystique that had always before filled her with joy? Instead, she felt awkward and ugly and just plain fat.

10

FERN WAS BOUNCING around, all excited. "Ooo, Jason, lemme see! Lemme see!"

Jason held out his hand and opened his fingers just enough for her to see inside.

"Ooo, where'd you find it?"

"In the water," said Jason.

Ugh, thought Cinni. Probably a condom, or something. She raised her head from the comfortable warmth of her beach towel, but couldn't see a thing. Jason was hiding it in his hand, whatever it was.

"Put it in water!" Fern squealed.

Cinni decided she had better intervene. "What have you got there, Jase?"

"A jellyfish," Fern called over her shoulder as she ran to the water's edge with Jason's red plastic bucket. She carried it back, slopping and dripping, took the object from Jason's hand and dropped it into the pail.

"I found it, so it's mine," Jason said, not irritably, but as a friendly reminder.

"It's both of ours, because I got the water," Fern informed him, quite matter-of-factly.

Just like Marilla and me, Cinni thought, remembering how she had always been able to manipulate the slightly younger girl. She had really been quite surprised when Marilla's stupid greed got in the way that last day.

And here was Fern, acquiring joint ownership of a jellyfish she had not found. If Cinni knew her children, it would soon be full ownership. It was domination not only by the bigger, stronger body, but by the bigger, stronger mind.

Just a matter of establishing authority, and you could make the little people dance.

She liked the idea of making little people dance. And big people, too.

Fern said, "Cinni, will you build another fort with us?"

Unhurriedly, Cinni sat up and stretched her back. Fern watched her and waited. Cinni nodded toward the sand, and Fern began digging.

After a moment, Fern looked up. "Do you know how to swim?"

Cinni laughed. "Sure I know how to swim. I wouldn't be much good at looking after you if I didn't know how to swim, would I?"

Fern did not know how to frame her next question. They both knew she was thinking of yesterday, but Cinni was not about to explain why she had done what she did. It had been very uncomfortable, but worth it, and that was the important thing.

Fern let it drop. She dug a little more, and then asked, "Do you have any brothers and sisters?"

"Nope," said Cinni. "What do I need brothers and sisters for?"

Fern looked surprised. Then, getting into the spirit of the thing, she wrinkled her nose at Jason. "I don't need them, either."

"You're going to have a whole mess of them," Cinni said. "Your mom's the breeding type."

"What does that mean?"

"Well—she's got one in her tummy right now. You know that?"

"I know it."

"That one will come out in a few months and you'll have a new baby brother or sister, and then I suppose there'll be another one after that, and an—"

"I can't wait for the baby!"

"I thought you didn't want brothers and sisters."

"I decided I do."

Fern's shovel struck a rock. It was a small one, dark muddy green with a crisscrossing of thin white lines that looked like plaid.

"That's pretty," said Cinny. "Can I have it?" She held out her hand.

Fern gave the rock one sad look, and then handed it to her. The next moment she was consoled by another find, a tiny opalescent yellow shell. She glanced warily at Cinni to see if Cinni would take that away from her, too, before she set it on top of the pool of water that had formed inside their fortress. "Look, a boat."

Cinni sniffed. "Whoever heard of a boat inside a fort? Maybe it's a reservoir. Sometimes people go fishing in reservoirs. Or other things float there. You know the reservoir in Central Park that's always covered with a million seagulls shitting up the water?"

Fern laughed, and Cinni smiled. She had known that would get her. Kids loved that kind of talk.

With no help from Cinni, the fort was completed. There was nothing more for any of them to do except watch the tide come in and wash it away. If you stopped to think about it, it really was kind of a drag sitting on the beach all day with a couple of kids, although that was better than sitting around home, lonely, bored, and broke. But this was only the first day. She had a whole summer. This day multiplied by approximately sixty.

Minus approximately fourteen gilt-edged, glamorous Saturdays and Sundays with Gavin.

He was not really gorgeous, like Pete, but he was cute, and he got to her somehow. She did not quite know how. He had brains, which Pete did not, and he was solid. On his way. His achievements would be more meaningful, and his life comfortable. She decided she wanted him instead of Pete.

She lay down on the towel, squeezing her thighs together. Four and a half days before she would see him again. They shouldn't do that to a poor girl, make her suffer like this. They ought to give him to her, all gift-wrapped and ready to go. Where are you, Santa Claus?

She wished now that she had not wasted that day with Pete.

She picked up the green plaid rock and tossed it and caught it a few times. It had a nice feel, smooth and round from ages of being knocked about in the ocean.

"Cinni, Jason's not staying under the umbrella."

"Jason," said Cinni, "you get the hell under the umbrella, do you hear?"

On the surface, her voice sounded calm, but there was something in it that made Jason obey.

Very good.

Fern continued to scrape listlessly at the basin of their fort. Her shell had long since sunk and she did not bother to retrieve it.

Cinni's eyes lighted on Jason's red bucket. She pulled it over to her and looked inside. There it was, just a blob of clear matter, like a piece of solidified water floating in the liquid water. She lifted it out and set it on the hard damp sand near her feet. It simply lay there, not even struggling the way a normal fish would. Holding the green plaid rock cupped in her hand, she smashed the jellyfish to pieces.

She had no time to observe the splattered, water-colored mess before a howl broke from the children.

"My jellyfish!" cried Jason in a hoarse roar.

"You killed it!" screamed Fern.

Cinni stared at them in astonishment. Jason's roar splintered into husky wails. Tears washed down his face, all suddenly, as if someone had turned on a water faucet.

"Why did you kill it?" Fern demanded shrilly. "*Why?*"

"Oh, come on," said Cinni. "What's the matter with you guys? It's only a dumb old jellyfish. It didn't even move."

"It was my jellyfish," Jason sobbed. "I wanted to keep it."

"Keep it for what?"

" 'Cause I wanted it!"

"Well, you haven't got it."

She could not believe these kids. Whoever heard of making a fuss over a jellyfish? A blob of transparent nothing.

"Why did you kill it?" Fern asked again, sniffling.

"Why not?" replied Cinni. "I just wanted to see what it would look like. Wasn't that funny, the way it went *squish*?"

Fern stared dully at where the *squish* had taken place, and shook her head.

Cinni said, "You guys are a couple of weirdos, if you want my opinion."

Fern's body shifted slightly, but she did not look at Cinni, or say anything.

"Come on, let's forget about the dumb jellyfish."

Still no reaction. She wondered if they would tell their mother. Not that there was any law against beating a jellyfish to death, but it might lead to some form of subtle propaganda against Cinni. She could see how the kids had been raised. She might have known Mary Shelburne was that kind of person.

"Jason, you look cute when you cry."

Jason raised his eyes, then lowered them quickly.

"Fern, you have a really beautiful suntan. Better than mine, even. Do you know, I think you two are the nicest, sweetest kids I ever took care of."

Grudgingly, Fern said, "Really?"

"Yes, really. I know a lot of kids, and you two are the best. I think I might even let you visit my island sometime."

A flicker of interest from Fern. "What island?"

"My island. My very own private island."

"Where is it?"

"Somewhere. And you can go sometime, if you're good. And if, Jason, you get back under that umbrella."

Jason got back under the umbrella. Fern asked, as

though Cinni had not heard her before, "Where is your island?"

"I can't tell you where it is, and no boats go there."

"Then how do you get to it?"

"I fly. Or swim."

"You can't fly without an airplane."

"I can. Do you know what my name is?"

"It's Cinni."

"That's what people call me, but my real name is Cynthia. Do you know what it means? It means 'moon goddess.' Naturally I don't go around telling people, only very special people, about me being a moon goddess. And I don't expect you to tell anybody, either."

"Are we special people?"

"I guess you must be, because I told you, didn't I?"

Garbage. She'd have done better to claim she was the tooth fairy. Of all the nauseating slop, but it got them where she wanted them. Jason had stopped bawling, the jellyfish had faded into past history, and they were both fascinated, if still just a little bit skeptical.

"When do you go there?" asked Fern.

"At night, when the moon's out. But you'll never see me go. I take my astral body, and leave my earthly one at home in bed, so nobody knows. But I have to be careful to get back in time, or people might find my earthly body and think it's dead, and bury it."

"Then you *would* be dead," said Fern.

"Well, I'd still have my astral body, but I wouldn't be able to appear in earthly form any more. So I'd have to stay on my island, and you'd never see me again."

"Who lives on your island?"

"I do. And people I like. People I invite. Nobody else."

"Are there any children?"

"Sometimes. If I invite them. But they have to be good. They can't give me any trouble. And I do mean that. *Any* trouble is too much. And one thing you have to remember is *never* tell anybody else, especially your mother. Don't tell anybody, is that clear?"

"Can't my mother go there?"

"Nope. No women. Only me. It's a rule I made. But," added Cinni, stretching out her legs and running a hand down her thigh, "someday I just might invite your daddy."

And then, she promised herself, we'll all live there together. The four of us.

Four, for a while.

Because if she had *them*, he would come, too. He wouldn't want to lose them. And he would see who was superior, if she could get them away from that tall, ashen-haired idiot. She would get everything away from her. He would see.

There was one other, sure way to make him her own. She would do that, too, closing off all avenues of escape.

She would get pregnant.

11

CINNI STOOD BY the kitchen sink, drumming her fingers and running a torrent from the hot-water tap.

"It won't get warm, Mrs. Shelburne, what's the matter with it? It's pure cold."

"Probably it needs a little longer to heat up after all those showers," Mary said. It had been a point of contention between them. Cinni had taken a thirty-minute shower, trying to wash all the salt out of her waist-length hair. Mary had had to show her the water heater, so she would understand how small its tank was.

"But it's been three hours," Cinni protested. "Do you think something could have happened to the heater?"

Mary felt her irritation beginning to rise again. "Just let the dishes go, Cinni. We can wash them in the morning."

"If the water's this cold now," Cinni argued, "the heater must have gone out, and there won't be any hot water in the morning, either. Do you want me to check?"

Without waiting for an answer, she opened the narrow door next to the bathroom and stood contemplating the object inside. She ran her hands over it, poking and prodding like a doctor. She turned on the hall light.

"Is this the switch here?" she called. "This red thing? It was turned to 'off.'"

"How could it be turned to 'off'?" Mary asked.

"I don't know, unless maybe you turned it by mistake when you were showing me earlier."

"I didn't even touch it."

"Well, actually you did. I'm a witness. Anyhow, it's all fixed now." Cinni closed the door. Tilting her head to one side, she smiled her charming smile and said fondly, "Honestly, Mrs. Shelburne, what am I going to do with you?"

Oh, hell, thought Mary. She had *not* touched it. She knew she hadn't. Not that it mattered, except for Cinni's patronizing attitude. She tried to calm her anger. She was overreacting.

Perhaps the children had done it. She must warn them to leave it alone. It was dangerous. She went to their room, and found them still awake, talking and giggling.

"Were either of you playing with the water heater?"

"What water heater?" asked Fern. They denied any knowledge of it.

As Mary turned to leave the room, Fern said, "Mommy, guess what. Jason found a jellyfish."

"Oh, what fun! What did it look like?"

"Like a piece of jelly, except it wasn't any color. We put it in his pail and we were going—"

She broke off. Mary turned to find Cinni smiling in the doorway.

"Everything okay?" Cinni said.

"Everything's marvelous," said Mary. "What were you starting to tell me, Fern?"

"Nothing."

Cinni brushed past Mary and went on into the room. "You kids had better get to sleep now. I already put you to bed once."

Fern held out her arms. "Cinni, kiss me goodnight."

Mary backed out of the room as the two girls embraced each other. It was good that the children accepted Cinni now. It hadn't taken long. Cinni knew how to win them over.

She wondered what Fern had been trying to tell her. It was something that bothered her, apparently. Something about Cinni?

Mary felt uneasy. Vaguely nagged. She could not think why. Everything was going smoothly, wasn't it? If Fern was bothered by something, it could not have been very important, for she seemed to forget it right away.

Something about the jellyfish?

She hoped Jason had put it back in the water, its familiar habitat.

Cinni gently closed the door to the children's room. "They'll be quiet now. Why don't you just take it easy, Mrs. Shelburne? I'll wash the dishes as soon as the water gets warm."

"I shouldn't let you," said Mary, "but I think I will. It would be so luxurious just to get in bed and read. I must have been born to be lazy."

And later, listening to the water splash as Cinni washed the dishes, she thought: That girl is the best investment I ever made.

She thought so again the next morning when, barely conscious at six o'clock, she heard Cinni's voice softly mingled with those of the children. There was an interval when the voices faded into the kitchen and Mary slept again, and then she was reawakened by a few nearby yelps and a vehement "Ssshh" from Cinni.

At eight o'clock she got out of bed, expecting to be surrounded by children frothing with impatience to go to the beach. Instead she saw them playing contentedly in back of the house. Cinni was in the kitchen, barefooted, wearing very brief white shorts that showed a long expanse of leg. She had not looked nearly so long-legged in April. She had not, in fact, looked like anything at all. Just a pleasant, competent girl in a blue dress with a Peter Pan collar. Perhaps it was the dress that detracted, made her appear chubby even when she wasn't. Or was dowdy the word?

"Cinni, did you lose weight since I first saw you?"

"I don't know. Do I look skinnier?" Cinni kicked out a leg and glanced at it briefly.

"A little."

"Then maybe I did. But you didn't see me like this, with practically no clothes on." She giggled and went back to wiping the kitchen table.

Mary cooked and ate her breakfast in relative peace, not even aware that Cinni had called the children in and changed them into their bathing suits. Odd, she thought as they shouted goodbye to her from the living room. They must have come through the front door. She wondered why, when the kitchen door was closer to where they had been.

She had dressed and was packing her camera bag when the back doorbell rang. It was Esther Reardon, in green shorts and a white tee shirt.

"You see?" she greeted Mary, "I'm not wearing pink. How would you like to come over for a cup of coffee?" Her quick eyes took in the camera bag. "You look as if you're going somewhere."

"Just out to take a few pictures. Photography used to be my hobby, and I'm all excited about getting back into it."

They agreed on the coffee first, and then she and Esther would go out together. Esther knew a lot of quaint spots. Quaintness was not what Mary sought, but it wouldn't hurt to have a guide who knew the area.

Esther's house was luxuriously air conditioned, a paradox of floor-to-ceiling windows and heavy drapes that covered the windows to keep out the hot sunshine. The living room was furnished in blue and green, with a sweeping modular couch that went around two walls, and a beige shag rug on the floor.

"How beautiful!" gasped Mary. "Esther, I love it. I love to see beautiful houses and imagine myself living in them. I mean, you can't live in every house you see," she tried to explain, flustered again by her spontaneous lunacy, "but you can have fun imagining different ones. It saves the trouble of having to rearrange your furniture just to get some variety."

"I know what you mean," said Esther. Did she? Probably she thought Mary was a nut.

Jack and the boys had gone out somewhere. After the two women finished their coffee, Esther picked up a shopping bag that held her crocheting, and they started out in Mary's car.

The first stop was a windmill just off the main street in town. Esther said it dated from the eighteenth century. She sat on her folding Tri-Pod chair, placidly crocheting an afghan in four shades of pink while Mary photographed the windmill from various angles.

"I like to take things against the sky," Mary explained, crouching in the grass near Esther's sandaled foot. "Then, when you print it, you can make beautiful sharp contrasts. It's always a dramatic effect."

They found a stone farmhouse that dated from the seventeenth century. It did not look as striking against the sky as the windmill had, but the sun and the trees created interesting shadows on it. Mary had to use a telescopic lens, for the house was inhabited, although they could not be sure whether or not the owners were home.

They took pictures of Block Island Sound and of Mattapogue harbor, and the lighthouse at Montauk Point. By the time they left Montauk it was two o'clock. Esther suggested they stop for lunch.

"I've really got to get back," Mary said. "It's so late. The children will be starving."

She need not have worried. The children had long since eaten their lunch and were resting on their beds while Cinni, in her own room, polished her fingernails.

"Hi, Mommy," Fern called out in a stage whisper.

"What's happening?" Mary asked. "You never do this at home."

"Cinni told us we had to rest, or we can't go to the beach this afternoon."

"I see."

So the girl had it all under control. Everything. The schedule, the meals, the children.

She was wonderful, that girl. Really wonderful.

12

THE CHILDREN WOULD love it. Mary thought, rising early to catch them before they could get ready for the beach.

Again they were sitting at the breakfast table as though the three of them belonged together. Their voices were silenced by her approach. She had the feeling that she was not quite welcome.

"Kids?" She spoke from the doorway. "Yesterday our next-door neighbor and I went all the way to Montauk Point. It's the very tip of Long Island, and there's a lighthouse there and a picnic ground. Shall we pack some sandwiches and go there today? We can see the lighthouse, play on the beach, have a picnic. . . ."

The children were silent. Fern inhaled sharply to expode into her usual "Oooo, yes!" but instead of exploding she turned to Cinni as though waiting for a cue.

Cinni wrinkled her nose. "Who wants to go to Montauk?" She glanced at Fern.

"Have you ever been there?" Mary asked.

"No, but I—" Cinni ducked her head, smiling sweetly. "I didn't mean to run down your offer, or anything. I mean, do you need me to go along? I'd rather stay here, if you don't mind. We were having such a good time at the beach yesterday."

"There's a beach at Montauk."

"Yes, but . . ." She sounded wistful.

Fern said, "I want to stay with Cinni."

"You've never seen a lighthouse," Mary argued. "*I* saw it yesterday. This trip was supposed to be for you."

She had wanted them to see it. She wanted to see it with them, and share their pleasure.

"Cinni doesn't have to go, of course. You deserve some time off, Cinni. You've been so conscientious."

"But I want to stay with Cinni," Fern repeated, and Jason echoed, "Me, too."

Mary retreated to her room. She wanted to ask "Why? What has this beach to offer, with Cinni, that the beach at Montauk, and the lighthouse, which you have never seen, can't offer—(with me)?" But she would not demean herself to ask that. She would try to find out somehow, but she would never ask it directly.

She went out alone with her camera, and returned in the middle of the afternoon to an empty house. She walked down to the beach until she could see them, a little cluster which she recognized by the colors of the hair and bathing suits, and the brown of Cinni's back. They seemed to be doing nothing but sitting idly, dabbling in the sand. Why was that better than a trip to Montauk?

The next day it rained. She was shocked. The first few days had been so bright and beautiful, she had not even remembered that it *could* rain.

She was half dressed when the door to her room flew open. "Mommy, can we play outside in the rain?"

It was both children, wide-eyed and eager. Mary said the first thing that occurred to her. "Why do you want to?" Rain was cold and soggy. But she should have remembered that it was different for children.

"I brought along some games for days like this," she told them, "and some old magazines and catalogs that you can cut up. I used to cut the figures out of Sears, Roebuck catalogs and make paper families. I'd cut out furniture, and make little houses with rooms. . . ."

She was winning them. She saw it in their eyes. At

that moment Cinni came up behind them, sliding a hand around each child.

"Aw, Mrs. Shelburne, it's fun to play in the rain. They wanted to so much."

"Yes, Mommy," said Fern.

Cinni added quickly, "I'll go with them and make sure they don't get cold."

She didn't mean to do it, Mary told herself, after she had given an almost inaudible assent. Naturally Cinni did not deliberately oppose her, or try to turn the children away from her. She was only a little too eager to perform her job, as she saw it. Perhaps that was the mistake in hiring one so young: an imbalance of emotion, or something like that. An imbalance of something, anyway. Still, it would have to be stopped. This tug-of-war could only damage the children.

But there were good times, too. There was the companionship she had looked forward to. In the evenings after the children had gone to bed, and she and Cinni washed the dishes together, or sat around the living room, they would talk. She realized that Cinni had no one else to talk to, and really needed her.

"Mrs. Shelburne, what's it like being married?"

"Good heavens, Cinni, what a complicated question."

A little laugh. "No, I didn't mean—That would be hard to answer, wouldn't it? No, actually, what I meant was, I just can't see myself being stuck with one guy for my whole life, there are so many nices ones in the world. Did you ever get attracted to anybody else, even after you were married?"

"No, I can't say that I did."

Oh, but she sounded priggish. And the girl was quite serious. Young people asked questions like that because they honestly wanted to know, as some sort of guideline for their own lives.

"Actually, somebody did make a play for me once, and in a very mild way, I kind of fell for it. Nothing happened, of course, but it was fun just having it to think about."

Still priggish. But it was the truth. What else could she say?

Her audience was riveted. Cinni's lips moved and she repeated in a whisper, "made a play for you." Then, louder, "That's another thing that's worried me—if something like that happens. People do it all the time to a single girl, but there are a lot of guys who don't seem to care if you're married, or if they are. What are you supposed to do?"

"Well, heavens, you just politely but firmly turn him off."

Cinni looked embarrassed, and again came out with a tiny laugh.

"I must sound like an idiot, asking that, but I was afraid I might get bored, or have a fight with my husband, and then if somebody went after me, I'd be awfully tempted."

"How, at your age, would you know anything about temptation?"

Cinni seemed not to hear her, and Mary was glad. It had been a very pompous sort of question. What was the matter with her this evening?

Cinni went on, addressing the ceiling: "You see, I keep thinking it might be awfully hard to live with somebody all the time like that. Don't you ever get on each other's nerves?"

Mary smiled, determined to be more helpful than she had heretofore been. In a way, it was a tribute that Cinni had turned to her. These were questions she could not even ask her own mother, who, in the first place, would probably wonder what her daughter was up to, and retaliate with a lot of questions of her own, and in the second place, did not herself seem very skillful at making marriage work, having run through two husbands already.

"Yes, of course we get on each other's nerves." It would not do to lead the girl into thinking that perfection was possible.

"How?"

"Well, to begin with, I think Gavin gets annoyed at my preoccupation with the children. The trouble is that children just do take a lot of time and attention, and there are only a certain number of hours in the day, but still, it's hard on a man. And I'm afraid it goes in a circle. He gets preoccupied with his job, and I get annoyed with what it's doing to him—"

"How do you mean?"

"Oh, just that—in any corporation they have a certain set of values and priorities that seem awfully stuffy and materialistic to somebody who's not involved. We used to have so much fun together. We used to read poetry together and go on photographing expeditions. Now he's just so—stuffy." She hated to use the same word twice. "The whole thing is a climb in status and responsibility. That's all he cares about. So it makes me even more immersed in the children, because that's all I have."

Cinni picked at her nail polish.

"Yes, I think I understand, Mrs. Shelburne. I'd probably resent that, too."

"I don't exactly resent it, but—"

"What was that other person like? The one you said you were attracted to for a while?"

Mary felt her face whiten. "Let's not make a big thing over that. As I said, nothing came of it."

"Well, I don't think it's particularly unusual anyway. But what was he like? Was he different?"

"Oh, yes. He was an artist. He did collage paintings, and things like that. A very free-wheeling spirit. That was probably one reason I liked him. But, please—"

"Oh, I'll forget it right away, Mrs. Shelburne. But—" Cinni smiled and buffed her nails on her shorts. "It does make me look at you a little bit differently."

13

AFTER THEY LEFT for the beach that Friday morning, Mary returned to her bed with a book. She did not feel like taking pictures.

In less than twelve hours, Gavin would be coming. Perhaps she would get a hold on things with Gavin there.

A hold on what things? She was not sure. Something was slipping away from her, and she did not quite know what it was. The children, perhaps. Her own children were not hers any more. Cinni, in an effort to be helpful and obliging, had managed to absorb them, as an amoeba absorbs its—not its prey, exactly. Its sustenance.

Cinni was in charge. Definitely. Not only of the children, but of everything, including Mary.

It had started with the water heater. Mary was certain she hadn't turned it off, but every now and then her certainty wobbled a little. And there were other things. The worst was Fern's bathing suit—the red bathing suit she had bought at Gimbels on that warm spring day. She did not see how it could have disappeared. It broke her heart, Fern's, too. Cinni insisted that it must have gone out with the trash, and it was Mary who had bundled up the trash. Impossible not to notice a bright red bathing suit among the newspapers, but what could she do? It was not to be found, and now Fern blamed her for its loss.

She looked up at the sound of a car's engine. Somebody was parking out there, next to her station wagon.

Puzzled, she closed the book, quickly got up from her unmade bed, and went to the door.

It was a dark green van. A young man, blond and bronzed and extraordinarily handsome, was getting out of it. He saw her standing at the screen door.

"Hi, is Cinni here? Cinni Ricks? Is this the right house?"

"This is the right house," said Mary, "but Cinni's not here just now. She's probably down at the beach. Are you a friend of hers?"

"My name's Pete Mitchell. I'm a friend from back home."

Mary held open the door to admit him. She could not help staring. A friend from back home, quite a hunk of man, and twenty-five if he was a day.

"A family friend?" It was none of her business, but Cinni was only a child, and in her care.

"No, just Cinni's friend." He grinned easily.

Good grief, thought Mary. She did not really know the circumstances. Cinni did seem like a competent young person. Yet only fourteen.

"Down at the beach, you say?" he prompted.

"Yes, she's there with my children. I'll show you where they usually go."

She was barefooted, but the sand was not yet hot. She felt disheveled. Who would have expected a visitor at this hour? But it would have been foolish to stop and fix her hair and put on lipstick. Hardly anybody was on the beach. There was no one to see her—except this Pete.

Cinni watched them coming. She did not move from her curled-up sitting position, her head resting on one bent knee."

"Hi, Cinni," Pete called as they approached.

She waited until he drew closer, then raised her head. "What are you doing here?"

"What do you think I'm doing? I came to see you. Brought my surfboard."

"Oh, Christ."

Mary glanced at Pete to see how he was taking this less-than-friendly reception. It had not yet erased his dazzling grin.

He stood over the girl, and spoke as though no one else was there. "What's the matter? Something bothering you?"

"No, nothing. You could have at least called."

Mary recollected the talk of a boyfriend. She had pictured, if anything, a fifteen-year-old. But this? And in front of her children?

They were gaping at the visitor. She reached out for them. "Fern and Jason, let's go back to the house."

Now they gaped at her. "Why?" asked Fern.

"So Cinni can talk to her friend. Come on."

"But I want to stay with Cinni."

"Fern, did you hear me?"

Out of embarrassment, she had spoken more sharply than she meant to. Fern gasped and, figuratively, dug in her heels.

Cinni said, "It's okay, Mrs. Shelburne, they can stay with me. We get along, don't we, kids?"

"When I tell them something—" Mary began.

"But I want them to stay, and they want to. Pete doesn't mind, do you, Pete?"

Mary took a step backward. What now? She strongly suspected that further discussion would only lead to further defeat. How could this be happening? She was their mother. Her word was law. Until now.

She turned quickly and went back to the house, alone. She ought to have said something. Wished them a nice time, or something, so she would not appear a bad loser. Or a loser at all, in fact.

She made her bed and tried to read, but the book no longer interested her. What could she do to get her children back? Cinni had wooed and won them somehow. Ordering them to return to her simply would not work. *She* would have to woo and win, but how?

She could fire the girl. That was all she really needed

to do, just fire the girl. But what explanation could she
give?

An hour later she walked partway back to the beach
to check on her children. They were not where she had
left them. After a moment of panic, she saw them over
on a side of the beach where nobody ever swam. They
were sitting in a row with Cinni in the middle, watching
Pete far out in the water, crouched on a surfboard.

She wondered how long he would wait there. It
seemed forever. Then suddenly the water swelled into a
wave larger than the others, and he rose to his feet and
was riding in toward shore. The children clapped. Cinni
stood up and danced, and when she did, they stood up
too. It was like watching a silent home movie. Mary
could see the clapping and dancing, but could not hear
them. Cinni danced across the sand to meet Pete, and after a brief discussion, took the surfboard from him and
waded into the water. Mary watched her paddle outward and crouch, waiting, as Pete had done. But Cinni
was clumsy. Perhaps her timing was off. She caught a
wave all right, but after a few seconds she toppled over
and had to retrieve the board by swimming after it.
Despite her failure, her children clapped and danced as
they had done for Pete. Mary went back to the house.

She puttered about, straightened the living room, and
counted her money to see whether she could afford
more film. But she dared not leave the house to go and
buy any. Cinni and Pete might want to go out somewhere, and she had to stay home to receive the children.

In another hour they returned from the beach. She
came from the bedroom to meet them, but all she found
was a dripping surfboard propped against the living
room wall, a bundle of wet towels on the floor, and the
sight of her children through the window, piling into the
back of Pete's green van and being driven away.

"Well! Thanks for asking," she said.

As the time went by, she began to feel anxious. The
children were so attached to Cinni, who could tell how

far they might follow her? What if Pete decided to go
back home with his entourage?

He wouldn't. No one would be that irresponsible. But
what if they suddenly barreled off to Cape Cod, or
someplace? She had assumed they were only going to
lunch, but lunch did not take three hours, even at the
slowest of fancy French restaurants, and as far as she
knew, they were still in their bathing suits, so she had
thought it would be more on the order of McDonald's.

She advised herself not to worry. It wasn't good for
the baby. It could spread poisoned juices all through her
body. But the children would follow Cinni to the
moon. . . .

When she thought she might go mad, they returned.
The doors of the van opened, disgorging her loved ones,
and then she felt guilty that she had been concerned for
the children and not for Cinni.

Pete opened the back of the van and pulled something
out. It was long and yellow and shiny. A surfboard. Fern
and Jason watched, clapping and dancing, as they had
done on the beach.

They brought the surfboard into the house and Fern
screamed to her mother, "Look what Cinni got! Now
we can go surfing, too!"

"How nice," said Mary. "But I wish you'd told me
where you were going."

All except Pete were eating ice cream cones. Around
her cone, Cinni said, "Aw, Mrs. Shelburne, you know
the kids are all right with me. I hope you didn't worry."

"Well, I did."

"Aw, that's a shame. If I knew you were going to
worry—We just went out to get my surfboard, and then
we drove around. We found the most beautiful place
over on the other side. It was absolutely deserted, just a
rocky point with its own little beach, and pine
trees. . . ."

"How could you be sure it wasn't part of an estate?"
Mary asked.

"I don't think so. It wasn't posted, there was nothing

around. You should go there sometime, Mrs. Shelburne, really, you'd like it. You could take pictures, and there's nobody to bother you."

"And there's this island—" Fern began. She stopped. The eagerness faded and her face became closed. Mary turned to find Cinni smiling at her.

"Yes, there's some real nice islands out there," Cinni said. "We'd have stayed, except there aren't any waves for surfing."

They tried out Cinni's new surfboard, and then came back to the house and took long showers that used up all the hot water. Mary set the table for dinner—a more elaborate dinner than they had had all week, because it was Gavin night. She wondered if Pete was staying. She ought to just ask, but somehow that seemed rude, as though she expected him not to stay. She set a place for him anyway.

Cinni and Pete sat on the living room sofa, murmuring in low voices. When Mary passed through on her way from the children's room, they seemed to fly apart from some close tangle, and Cinni glanced at her guiltily.

That *child*. Did her mother know about this man? Mary wondered how far her own responsibility went.

She was putting the finishing touches on a vegetable casserole when Cinni same into the kitchen.

"I forgot to tell you, Mrs. Shelburne, we're eating out. I noticed you set six places."

"I wasn't sure," said Mary.

"I know, it's my fault. I forgot to tell you."

Pete came up behind Cinni and slid his hand around her neck, catching hold of her ear. She jerked herself away and flushed slightly. With a brief, embarrassed smile at Mary, as though to say "You know how men are," she went back to the living room.

Mary felt like a shuttle. First down the hall to the children, to supervise the putting on of their shoes so they could go with her to the station. Then to the kitchen. . . .

Pete and Cinni had their heads together once again

and were whispering. A distinct phrase reached her ears—"I felt sorry for your wife—"

"Good God, a wife? And this, the other woman? Impossible. What, again, were her responsibilities as mother-in-residence?

Responsibilities be damned. She had a temptress in her home. A Lorelei, who had already taken her children. How could she have suspected, back there at the interview?

Not even now would she suspect it. It was too ridiculous. She must have misunderstood everything—the remark, their relationship, the springing guiltily apart.

Back again for the children, and to get her purse and car keys.

"Cinni, we're just running down to the station to pick up Gavin."

Fern stopped dead in the middle of the living room. "Isn't Cinni going?"

"Cinni has a guest," Mary reminded her.

"Then I don't want to go."

"Fern! Don't you want to see Daddy?"

"I want to stay with Cinni."

"Me, too," said Jason.

Cinni watched the scene with mild interest. Finally she spoke. "That's okay, Mrs. Shelburne, they can stay. We won't leave till you get back."

"Children, I really think—"

But Fern had sat down on the sofa next to Cinni and wound her arms around her.

Jason, with few original ideas, followed suit. But as both sides of Cinni were now taken up with Fern and Pete, he had to sit on her lap.

Cinni, gratified and laughing, raised her head from the smothering affection long enough to make a sisterly face at Mary. *Aren't kids the limit?*

"Daddy will be disappointed," said Mary, and went out to the car, being careful not to let the door slam behind her, lest she appear childish. She roared the engine, backed around recklessly, nearly hitting Pete's van, and

drove away with a spinning of wheels and splattering o
pebbles. She *was* being childish. Why take it out on th
car? But it made her feel better.

Gavin was in a good mood.

"How are you, sweetheart? Feeling okay? What have
you been doing all week?"

She told him about her photography, and about Esther. Somehow it did not sound very interesting.

"How are the kids?" he asked. "And your little
helper?"

"The kids are fine. Quite enamoured of the little
helper, who has some kind of boyfriend visiting."

"A what?"

Did she detect a sharp edge to the question?

"A boyfriend, cum surfboard. I only hope he's not
spending the weekend."

Gavin said nothing. She supposed there was nothing
really to say. When they entered the house, it was again
to find Pete and Cinni becoming instantly disentangled
from each other, and then standing up from the sofa in a
flurry of surreptitious hair-and-clothes straightening and
awkward smiles of greeting. Mary turned to Gavin as
she performed introductions. Gavin's face was dark and
closed and his manner vague.

He might have been more polite, she thought as she
went to the kitchen to put her casserole in the oven, but
his lack of warmth was not really what bothered her.
She thought she probably knew what really bothered
her, but did not want to admit it to herself.

Almost immediately, Pete and Cinni gathered up their
surfboards, called goodbye, and went out to the van.

Fern and Jason rushed to the door and stood looking
through the screen like two abandoned puppies. Cinni
waved her hand. " 'Bye, kids, I'll see you later."

"Aw-w-w," exclaimed Fern, not loudly enough for
Cinni to hear her.

Mary called from the kitchen, " Fern, why don't you
tell Daddy what you've been doing all week?"

Fern replied dully, "Playing on the beach." Then she

warmed to talking about today, and surfing, and Cinni's new surfboard, and the trip they had taken with Cinni and Pete, and Cinni in general.

"I told you they were enamoured," Mary said to Gavin. He regarded her blankly.

Beginning with dinner, the evening seemed unusually quiet. Mary could not think why. There were the same people who gathered together every evening at home in the city, and there it was lively and at times noisy, so that she always felt relieved once she had the children in bed and could sit down and read, if she still had the energy.

But here—what was wrong? Perhaps it was the lack of television. And yet at home the set was not always turned on. Perhaps it was that the children appeared aimless and subdued—in Cinni's absence. Why did they need Cinni? They had never heard of her before last spring, and they had managed all right.

Gavin, too, was subdued, too preoccupied to speak much to Mary, although she tried telling him about some of the attractive spots she had photographed. He had brought an attaché case full of work to do over the weekend, but it sat untouched in the bedroom while he paced up and down the tiny house, if anything, more aimless than the children.

"Would you like to go out for a walk or a drive?" Mary suggested. He shook his head.

"Is something bothering you about the office?"

Again he shook his head.

"It's silly to come all the way out here, and then act as if you wish you weren't here," she said. "Do you wish you weren't here?"

"It's okay, Mary, don't worry about me. No, I don't wish I weren't here."

Too many negatives. She assumed that he meant he didn't mind being there, but he seemed to mind something very much. When he asked one or two questions about Pete, she began to get a blurry picture of what it might be.

"Yes, of course he's much older than she is," she replied, "and furthermore, I think he might be married. I heard Cinni tell him something about, quote, 'your wife.'"

Gavin's hands clenched into fists.

At midnight, Gavin wondered aloud where "they" were. It was kind of late to be surfing, he said.

"Maybe they went somewhere after surfing," Mary remarked. She put on her nightgown and got into bed to read.

Gavin dickered with the radio, trying to catch some news. Most of it was local and uninteresting. If a revolution erupted in Africa, probably they would mention it last, after the firemen's fund-raising drive, and the boat that turned over in Shinnecock Bay.

She began to grow sleepy. She struggled on for a few more minutes, then rearranged her pillows and lay down.

"Gavin, would you mind? If you don't like what's on the radio, you might as well turn it off."

He was switching stations constantly, so that the sound came out in yips and squawks.

"You know," he said, "I feel responsible."

"For what?"

"For her. The girl."

"I suppose, in a way, you are, and so am I. I'm sorry I brought all this on you, Gavin."

He turned the radio dial again, but he had lowered the volume.

What made him think Cinni was not all right? They were certainly responsible for her life and limb, but were they also responsible for her virginity? Perhaps they were. And at fourteen . . . But Cinni had known Pete before she came under their care. It was not as if he was their fault.

What had become of the little nun in white shoes?

Mary slept for a while, and then woke.

"Gavin, it's two o'clock."

"They went out with a *surfboard*, for Christ sake. My God, Mary, what do we tell her mother?"

So that was it. What if something *had* happened?

"It was daylight when they went out," she said. "They wouldn't still be surfing."

"That's just what I mean." He began pulling on his trousers.

She sat up. "Where are you going? I'm sure they're all right, Gavin. Pete's, after all, a grown-up. And you don't even know where to look."

"I've got to be doing something." With jerky motions, he tied on his sneakers. "Fern mentioned some kind of point. I'll try there."

"But you don't know where the point *is*," said Mary. "And what if they're there and they don't want you?"

He paused, for an instant frozen. And in that instant she knew for certain that it was not Cinni's actual safety he was worried about.

She ought to worry, too. A fourteen-year-old child in her care, out all night with a married man. Good lord.

And yet Cinni seemed competent enough to handle even Pete. Mary felt sure nothing would happen to her that she did not want to happen, and if she wanted it, who could stop her?

Gavin had gotten the other shoe on, and stood up. "What if they're in trouble?"

Her thoughts raced ahead without him. "If they've drowned, they've already done it," she sighed, willing to go along with the pretense that *that* was what bothered him.

He hesitated, reluctant to make a fool of himself.

She said, "If they aren't back by morning, then it would make sense to go and look."

He took his car keys from the top of the dresser. "I'm going."

After he left, Mary lay down again in the peace of the house. But she was wide awake, haunted by a fear which she tried not to acknowledge.

Why did he worry so much? Didn't young people often stay out half the night? Or all of it? His was an angry worry, and in truth, it was not worry at all. It was jealousy. He had been prepared to hate Pete right from the beginning.

But how? Why? Was Gavin out of his mind? *A fourteen-year-old girl?*

She lay awake, feeling as though someone had scooped out her insides. What did you *do* in a case like this?

Dear Abby: My husband has flipped over our fourteen-year-old babysitter. . . .

If Dear Abby could solve it, Mary should be able to, too.

Maybe I'm the one who's crazy, she thought. Of course he feels responsible for her. It's like having another daughter in the house. Maybe I'm the one who's shirking responsibility, not caring enough.

He returned at three-thirty, alone. She pretended to be asleep as he came into the room and lay down on his bed, fully dressed.

He was restless, twitching and tossing and squeaking the bedsprings. He wanted to wait there and not be seen, in case they should come home. But he could not relax. Did he really think they had drowned?

She lay, also not sleeping, but forcing herself to breathe as though in sleep. She did not want him to talk to her.

She must have lain there, she thought, for about a year, listening to Gavin fidget and fume, when a car slowly approached, its headlights casting patterns on the wall. It came to a stop just outside the house.

Gavin muttered, "Four o'clock, for Christ sake. Damn punk."

And Mary knew she had been right.

14
∽

THEY DID NOT hear his car drive away, but when they woke in the morning, Pete had gone. Thank heaven. Gavin's mood returned to normal.

In the middle of the morning they all went out to the beach. Cinni took her surfboard, which necessitated their sitting away from the other swimmers. Gavin overcame his usual inhibitions about appearing less than perfect before his fellow humans, and allowed Cinni to teach him how to use the board. On his first trip out with it he did better than Cinni herself, riding it gracefully and staying on it longer.

"Wow, Gavin, you've got natural talent," she exclaimed, and he grinned, his teeth showing whiter than ever against his deepening tan.

Mary felt old and dowdy, sitting with the children, in her maternity swimdress. It was full and skirted and black with a pink and blue morning-glory design. An old-lady suit. It had looked pretty in the store, but she wished now that she had gotten a brighter color.

"Jason, stay under the umbrella," she murmured absently.

"I want to ride on the surfboard."

"I could take him out with me," Gavin offered, standing over Mary like a muscular god.

"On a surfboard? Are you crazy?"

"Just sitting on it. I wouldn't try riding the waves with a kid. You should know that."

"Gavin, he can't even swim, and that's *surf* out there."

"Maybe you're right." Uninterested, Gavin turned away, drying and combing his hair.

At that moment Cinni fell off the board and got a thorough ducking. Gavin ran to meet her and to rescue the board. He brought her over to their camp and patted her back while she choked and sputtered.

"You'd better let yourself dry out for a while," he advised.

"I think it's dangerous," said Mary. "How often do surfers drown?"

Over the top of Cinni's head, Gavin's eyes connected with hers. Perhaps he was remembering last night. She had not even thought of last night when she said it.

"If you're all going to stay here for a while," she said, "maybe I'll get myself wet." Entrusting the children to their father and babysitter, she waded into the sea.

It was achingly cold, but she would not turn back. She plunged in up to her shoulders and swam toward the far horizon. When she thought she had gone enough distance to make Gavin notice her, she changed direction and swam parallel to the beach.

It was appalling how little stamina she had when she was pregnant. There seemed to be no reserve of energy. She felt a moment of panic when she was exhausted and could not touch ground with her feet, but she managed to float, rising and falling on the swells, until she drifted in to shore and could walk the rest of the way.

She emerged, dripping, from the water and hurried to get a towel. Fern looked up from the hole she was digging and gave her a busy smile. Jason had filled his plastic bucket with clam shells, and would probably want to keep them forever. Gavin sat crosslegged on the sand, talking animatedly to a rapt and oiled Cinni.

Mary sat down, shivering and swathed in the towel. She was like a cloud shadow passing over them, making them only subliminally aware of her presence.

After a while Cinni turned to her lazily. "Wow, Mrs. Shelburne, where did you learn to swim like that? You're really good." Despite the enthusiastic words, her voice was flat and vague.

"Thank you," said Mary. "I suppose it was camp."

Gavin elaborated. "Mary went off to camp every summer when she was a kid. Never missed a year. Even got to be a swimming counselor after a while, didn't you, Mary?"

Mary sniffed. "You make it sound as if it was voluntary." To Cinni, she explained, "It was not voluntary. My parents made me go, and then they went off on a glamorous holiday by themselves. I hated the damn place."

"You were an only child?" Cinni asked. Mary nodded.

Gavin said, "You should be glad they sent you. Look at what you got out of it. Isn't it nice to have something you can do really well?"

He did not realize what it sounded like. Was that *all* she was good for?

Some people, she reflected from under a wave of paranoia, can't do anything well, yet they still count as people.

She watched Jason with his shells and Fern with her shovel, and thought how precious they were. She would always keep her family together. They would always share their good times. Unless, of course, the children wanted to go away sometime. It would have to be their decision, not hers.

She had, in fact, before the threatened loss of Christopher (or Daphne), looked forward to this summer with just Fern and Jason and herself, taking walks with them, reading poetry, and dreaming of Cape Cod or the Canary Islands, or even Mattapogue.

It would have been perfect.

Then, when she knew she would need someone else, she had been so happy that it was Cinni, but now the happiness was wearing off.

After a while she felt the sun begin to scorch her skin.

Dreading another burn, she went back to the house while the others remained on the beach. They must have had hides made of leather. And the endurance of long-distance runners. She looked out sometime later and saw them surfing again.

When they finally came into the house, she presented them with a cold lunch. But before Cinni could eat, she had to wash the salt out of her hair.

"Won't your hair get terribly dry with all that washing?" Mary asked her as she disappeared into the bathroom.

"Sure it will. That's why I have to condition it. But, see, the salt dries it even worse, and leaves it gummy."

She emerged half an hour later, demure in white shorts and tee shirt, with a towel around her head. Smiling absently at Mary, she went out the back door, taking a kitchen chair with her, and sat in the sun to dry her hair.

It was a sensual performance. She leaned back, tilting the chair on two legs, her eyes closed as she bathed in the sunshine. She played with her hair, holding it in her hand and flopping it, draping it over one shoulder, then over the other, lifting it and letting it fall, winding it around her head.

Mary, cleaning up after lunch, became aware of Gavin looking out through the kitchen window while he pretended to lean innocently against the refrigerator, drinking a beer.

Mary said, "She has beautiful hair. It's turning almost platinum in the sun."

Gavin started, frowned, and jerked away from the refrigerator. Casting about for distraction, he asked, "How are you feeling these days?"

"All right, I guess."

"No more bleeding?"

"No, it's okay, and it kicks a lot. We may be out of the woods."

The baby was all right, but Mary felt almost constantly tired. It was sleepiness more than physical fatigue, and with Cinni there, she could indulge herself. She went to bed that night at nine o'clock. They told her it was much too early. She reminded them that she was sleeping for two.

She woke in the middle of the night, or something that felt like the middle. She turned the clock so that it faced her. It was really only twelve-thirty.

Gavin's bed was still empty. He often stayed up late, but she thought the house seemed unnaturally quiet. She got up and opened her bedroom door. In the hallway, the children's door was closed, as it should have been. Cinni's stood open and her room was dark.

Mary went into the living room. One lamp burned, and a faucet dripped in the kitchen.

Where could they be, Cinni and Gavin, at twelve-thirty in the morning?

She went back to bed, remembering the way Cinni had dried her hair that afternoon, and the way Gavin had watched her.

And the way Gavin had worried when Cinni was out with Pete.

She rejected it at once. Cinni was only a child, for heaven's sake. Almost twice the age of Gavin's own daughter. Gavin *wouldn't*. He was not that kind.

She knew it could happen. She was not without sophistication.

But not Gavin. There had been a time when she could read his soul, and he just wouldn't.

She lay in bed, staring up at the darkness, and wondered where on earth they could be.

15

GAVIN HELD HER hand as they climbed over the dunes. She had tripped once and almost fallen. It was hard to see the clumps of roots in the darkness.

"I love it at night, don't you?" Cinni's voice was high and childish. "I think I was made for night. A lady of the night."

"That has a special meaning that maybe you don't know about," Gavin told her.

"Like what?"

"Never mind."

"Oh, shoot, maybe I can guess." She giggled with amusement at her own mistake. "I'm sorry." She stumbled again, and his hand tightened on hers.

"Maybe I'd better slow down," she said, and slowed, giving his hand a reassuring squeeze.

"I wanted to ask you something, Gavin. Does pregnancy make people absent-minded?"

"Not that I know of. Why?"

"Well—I don't know, I hate to say this, except it bothers me. I get worried that something really serious might happen. I mean—"

"What *do* you mean, Cinni?"

"I guess I shouldn't have brought it up, but you know, so many dumb little things happen. I mean dumb because they don't seem important."

Impulsively she drew closer and linked her arm

through his. He thought she probably did it unconsciously. She had a very physical way of relating. Not at all like Mary, whose instinct was more often to withdraw from people. Physically, at least. Of course Mary'd been brought up by a couple of rather elderly cold fish. She'd overcome that handicap and turned into a warm, human person. A beautiful person. But she didn't use her body the way this girl did. She didn't know how.

"Well, anyway," the girl was saying, "it's these little things like accidentally turning off the water heater so we couldn't take baths, or forgetting to buy something she promised the kids. And then Fern had this darling little red swimsuit, and one day it just disappeared. We never found it. I could have sworn I saw something red in the bundle of newspapers we put out with the garbage, but I didn't think of going out and looking, not then. That was before we missed the suit. I mean, it's little things like that, but it bothers me. I just love her, and I hate to say anything, but honestly, she's so scatterbrained I get scared something might happen to the kids."

He balked at the word "scatterbrained." He had never known Mary to be scatterbrained, but she certainly did have a penchant for daydreaming. For all he knew, the hormone changes in pregnancy could make it worse. Or maybe, even though she didn't let on, she was still torn up with fear of losing the baby, and it preoccupied her thoughts.

"I'm sorry it's causing you trouble," he said a bit gruffly, "but I don't think you need to worry. She'd never let anything happen to the kids."

"Oh, that's good." Relief poured into Cinni's voice. "I mean, I know part of the reason she hired me was that she didn't trust herself, you know, because of this pregnancy, so I got worried."

"It's all right, Cinni."

"Yes, because she told me about some of her strange behavior, so I just wondered." Cinni paused and looked out at the moon path on the water. "Isn't that just the most beautiful thing?"

"What strange behavior?" he asked.

"Oh, you know, that artist she fell in love with a couple of years ago, or whenever it was. She said she was afraid she neglected the kids. I didn't know how often she did this sort of thing. That must be almost a full moon, right?"

"It's a waxing gibbous," he said absently. "It'll be full in a few days."

"Oh, I wish you could be here to see it. Do you know which day?"

"What do I need a full moon for? I'm not a werewolf. Are you?" He wondered how he could banter like this, after what she had just told him.

"Oh, *Gavin.*" She ducked her head, giggling. She was still holding his arm. "I just like to look at it, it's so beautiful. You can't see the sky very well in the city."

"That's true."

He had to know more about this artist, but not from her. He didn't really want to ask Mary, either. Perhaps he was afraid to hear it confirmed.

His keeping silent would make Cinni think he knew all about it. She would think he and Mary had a marriage of convenience, and went their separate ways.

Hell, who cared what Cinni thought?

But she would go home and tell her mother, and her mother would think it was wicked that she had been exposed to such a lifestyle. He heaved a voiceless sigh.

"Are you getting tired, Gavin?"

"Me? Tired of what?"

"Tired of walking. I just wondered. You sounded tired."

"Not in the slightest. There are more ways of getting tired than just physically."

"That's what she said, too. That's why she went for the artist and those others. It was a sort of tiredness of— Oh, my *God*, Gavin, what am I *saying?*"

He gritted his teeth and calmly replied, "I can't imagine. What are you saying?"

"I didn't mean—Oh, I shouldn't say these things to *you.*"

"Preferably not to anybody else."

"I just forgot—Oh, you know, it's so lovely the way she and I can talk to each other, and confide things. I never had anybody like that before, and I forgot it was you we were talking about. Oh, me and my big mouth." She slapped herself across the face. It was a hard slap.

"Hey, stop that." He caught her wrist. "You'll knock your teeth out."

"I deserve it, for talking so much and hurting your feelings." She turned and looked into his eyes, both her hands holding both his arms. "Will you do me a favor, even if you hate me? Will you forget what I said?"

Was she wearing her contact lenses, he wondered? Her eyes in the moonlight were huge and bright.

He would certainly not forget what she had said, but he might, if he tried very hard, be able to ignore the fact that it was she who said it. It wasn't the saying of it that mattered so much.

"In the first place," he said, "why would I hate you?"

"For saying those things. Big blabbermouth me. I'm so tactless."

"It must be that moonshine out there." He nodded toward the heavenly body and its reflection on the water.

"I guess so," she answered in a tiny, contrite voice.

"Do you think we ought to start back?"

She hesitated. "Can we rest a little bit? My legs are ready to collapse." She sank down onto the sand. "Probably from all that surfing today."

Gavin sat down next to her. She began massaging her tired right leg, starting with the ankle and working upward. Gavin, so close beside her, wondered if he ought to help with the left leg.

She took off her sandals and stretched her legs in a catlike way, feeling every muscle.

Then she reached over and ran the flat of her palm across his knee. "Aren't you tired? You were surfing as much as I was. It really feels good if you do this."

She began at his ankle and massaged his leg as she had done her own. He was wearing Bermuda shorts and sneakers. It felt good, but not in the way she meant. He wondered how far up she would go.

Or did she mean it that way?

He groped cautiously.

"You're quite a girl, Cinni."

"I am?" The response was given rhetorically, without much apparent interest. But she eased herself over so that the nine-inch gap between them was closed, and she applied both her hands to the massaging of his leg.

His arm was in the way, so he put it around her. She rested her head on his shoulder. "Gavin, you feel so comfortable."

Now only her left hand was busy, working its way up his inner thigh.

That did it.

"Oh, man," he breathed, tightening his arm around her. He was beyond control. She struggled with his zipper, opened it and reached inside.

He ought to have stopped her, but he couldn't help himself. He was so ready. She knew what she was doing. He delayed only enough to give her a long kiss, allowing her to feel the inside of his mouth with her tongue. Then he pushed her back gently against the sand and removed her shorts.

In the moonlight her body glowed silver. Her hips were developed like a woman's. He gave no more thought to the fact that she was only a young girl. As he knelt over her, she unfastened the buckle on his shorts and slid them down over his legs.

"Oh, Gavin," she murmured, reaching up to pull him closer.

16

MARY WATCHED THE car drive away with all of them in it. Gavin had called to her, "We'll be back," and then taken the children and Cinni, and given no explanation as to what was happening.

She returned to setting the table for supper, but she felt rebellious. Gavin had spent the morning and a large part of the afternoon surfing with Cinni, and now they had gone off somewhere, and in about three hours he would be leaving. And Wednesday was her birthday. He would not be there, and he had not remembered or said one word about it all day. In fact, he had been rather oddly silent and stand-offish.

She felt rebellious enough to pour herself a glass of sherry and sit down with it instead of finishing the table. "Happy birthday to me," she said softly into the dead hot air of the living room.

The baby thumped inside her.

"Thank you, darling," she replied. "I'm glad you remembered."

What *was* the matter with Gavin? He had been so cold to her that day. With her birthday coming up, it was too terrible. She was sentimental about birthdays. They had nothing to do with growing older. She did not even think about that part of it. Her birthday was just her special day, the day on which she had been given to the world, and those who loved her ought to be nice to her.

It had started in the morning. She had thrown off her sheet, expecting him to get in bed with her. Instead he had lain where he was, and glowered, and made some crack about, "No wonder you don't have any spare time at home, with your busy social life."

She had chosen to ignore it, because it made no sense. What social life? Coffee maybe once a week with Lucille Wilkin, talking to the other mothers at the playground, but she didn't go there for that purpose. She only talked to them because she happened to be there with Jason. And sometimes she didn't go to the playground at all, but took Jason down to the river's edge with his tricycle. While he rode up and down the path, she would gaze northward at the Golden Horn. She would try to write poetry, but she was much better at reading than writing it.

She jumped up guiltily at the sound of the car. They had not been gone long. When they came into the house, Fern was carrying a bundle wrapped in a pink towel. She grinned with unconcealed pleasure and mischief, and Mary at once guessed that they had gone out to buy something for her birthday. Cinni and Jason were smirking, too. Only Gavin's look was grudging, but whatever he had against her, at least he had done the right thing. That was how Gavins advanced in the business world. No matter what their personal feelings, they always did the right thing. Still she wondered what he had against her—he, who had been unaccountably missing from the house at half-past-twelve last night.

What they had bought was a cake. They unveiled it just before the dessert course. It was a white cake with pink and blue sugar roses.

"Gavin, I thought you forgot," she told him over the smoke of blown-out candles. "You didn't say anything all day."

"But this isn't your real birthday," Fern reminded her,

'so he didn't have to say anything, but Daddy can't be here on your real birthday."

Mary looked forward to their drive to the station, when she could talk and perhaps find out what was bothering him. But when it came time to leave, Cinni herded the children out to the car.

As if she's part of the family, Mary thought with resentment.

Even on the platform, she hadn't a chance to be alone with him. Cinni and the children were all there, surrounding Gavin like a fan club. When the train came in, he squeezed Mary's hand, kissed Fern and Jason, and boarded.

On the drive home, Mary reminded herself how young the girl was. Young and ignorant. No doubt it never occurred to her that a married couple might want to say a private goodbye to each other. She had considerable poise, quite a bit of maturity, but much awkwardness still, that nun in white shoes.

Fern sat next to Mary in the front seat. Feeling her there, Mary knew a terrible yearning. She wanted them all to herself that summer, the way she always had them at home. Why Cinni? She could have managed without Cinni. It was not so strenuous here at the beach. And the baby was healthy and kicking vigorously. No apparent danger there. She could not have known, back in April, how it would be now, but she wished that, at this point, there were some polite way of getting rid of the girl.

As soon as they were home, Cinni took charge again. "Okay, kids, off to bed."

To Mary's surprise, the children resisted. It was the first time she had heard them dispute anything Cinni did or said, and it made her secretly happy.

Almost immediately, she realized that she had an obligation to back Cinni up. She started to speak, but before any words could come out, Cinni handled it deftly.

"All right, then, you get ready, wash your hands and faces and brush your teeth, while I do the dishes. If you're all ready and in your pajamas, I'll read you a story."

Fern let out one of her "Ooooooo's" and hurried to the bathroom. Mary said, "I'll wash the dishes, Cinni."

"Oh, no, Mrs. Shelburne, it's your birthday. I'll take care of it. You just sit down and enjoy yourself."

"It's not my actual birthday," Mary said. "And don't call me 'Mrs. Shelburne,' it sounds so stiff." She had noticed that Cinni called Gavin "Gavin."

Cinni did not argue when Mary took her place at the sink. But she was silent, standing there holding her towel. It was not like her. Ordinarily she chattered. She would tell Mary all her thoughts and problems, such as how dissatisfied she was at home, with her mother alternately nagging and ignoring her, and it would be so many years before she could legally move out, that she sometimes thought of running away.

Once Mary had said, "I'm sorry this job can't be more of a holiday for you," and Cinni had replied, "Oh, but it is. I love the job and I love Fern and Jason. I feel as if I have a place with them."

But tonight Cinni said nothing, in spite of the fact that she seemed uneasy and a bit fidgety, as though she wanted to speak.

Finally Mary asked, "Is something wrong, Cinni?"

"Oh . . . I don't know."

She had confided before. Why not now? Mary tried again. "If there's something on your mind, why don't we talk about it?"

"Well, there is something, but I don't know if—" Cinni broke off, her mouth twisting into a grimace. She rubbed one bare foot against her ankle.

"You don't know what?"

"If I should say it. I don't want to upset you."

"Why would it upset me?" *Maybe she's thinking of leaving*, Mary thought in sudden joy.

"Well, because—it's about Gavin."

"Oh?"

"He—I—I don't know how to say this, Mrs. Shelburne.

He—I think it was Saturday night, when you were asleep. He—tried—Well, he got a little fresh with me."

The last words came out in a rush, leaving Cinni looking wrung out.

Mary felt as though all her blood had drained away. Her head spun and she gasped, "I'm glad you did tell me."

How could he? How *could* Gavin? That was not the man she had always known. Not him at all.

"It isn't like him," she told Cinni. Her voice sounded unsteady. "Maybe he had a drink, or something. Was he drinking? Or maybe the office—under pressure. . . . I'm sure he wouldn't—"

A hand suddenly pressed her arm, and it was Cinni who comforted *her*.

"I shouldn't have said anything, Mrs. Shelburne, I'm really sorry. And almost your birthday, too. I shouldn't have told you. I should have kept it to myself, handled it myself."

Mary asked, "How could you? You're only fourteen. That's so young."

A kaleidoscope of images spun in her mind: Cinni drying her hair with those seductive body motions; Cinni's grown-up, married friend Pete, and the sophisticated way she handled him.

But she couldn't really be so sophisticated. Not if she reacted like this to Gavin. Her seductiveness was probably only a copy of something she had seen, and Gavin tumbled for it, not realizing it was nothing but a surface imitation.

How could he have been so stupid? Gavin was usually quite sharp. In that moment she hated him, hated all men for being spineless victims of their sex glands. No will of their own. No character. Just led around by the libido.

The telephone rang. "Oh, God," said Mary. That was all she needed—to have to talk to somebody now.

"Want me to answer it?" Cinni offered.

It rang again in its corner of the living room, and Mary went to pick it up.

"Hello, darling," said the voice at the other end. "This is Mary, isn't it?"

Oh, God. Martina. Why did it have to be his *mother* right now?

"How are you, Martina? Where are you calling from? Greece?" She was fond of her mother-in-law, even if Martina did have a fool for a son.

"Just got back. I'm with some friends in Great Neck. How about if I pop out for a short visit, say around Thursday?"

"Oh, lovely!" Mary cried, for a moment forgetting that they had no place to put her.

She forgot Gavin, too. For an instant she forgot all the horrible things that were happening.

But after she hung up and saw Cinni watching her, she remembered.

And remembered Gavin's coldness that day, his distance, and she felt cold herself.

Was it possible? Could he actually be falling in love with Cinni?

They were all in bed, Cinni liked it that way. Lucky for her that the pale, frail, pregnant one crumped out so early. That way, Cinni had the night to herself. A good thing, even without Gavin there. It gave her a chance to recharge her batteries.

She stretched out a leg and idly admired it, long and tanned and sexy. She stretched out both legs and ran her hand up and down her thigh. Some batteries! She took a sip of sherry from the glass in her other hand.

It had been a pretty good weekend, as weekends went. Of course she was at a disadvantage, having only the weekends. She might not be able to get it right for her fertile period, but at least she had started a relationship that could continue in the city.

And she had made an excellent beginning with those wedges she had driven between the two of them. Not bad at all, the way she had them dancing to her tune.

They were playing the whole thing her way, and they didn't even realize there was anything going on!

Already she had the kids completely in her hands. If she told them to walk into the ocean and drown, they would probably do it, just to please her. Kids were simple (in more ways than one). Gavin would take a little more work, but if she could just get pregnant. . . . She would cry and be terribly afraid of an abortion, afraid she might die, afraid God would punish her, and what could he do? Mary would get a nice settlement, and she could keep her damn baby. Fern and Jason, naturally, would want to go with Cinni. That suited her purposes for now. Later she would worry about what to do with them.

She closed her eyes, sipped her sherry, and listened to the night. All you could hear in that place was surf. No cars, no sirens, no bottles crashing out of tenth-floor windows. This was Mary's world. It pleased Mary. Even the city pleased Mary. Cinni had rarely seen anyone so damned pleased. No, a better word—satisfied. Maybe even "happy." Cinni had noticed it the very first time she saw her.

But not for long. It wouldn't be Mary's much longer. The end was already in sight. Look how Gavin had behaved all day, just because of what Cinni told him. Pretty putty Gavin.

She stood up, smoothed her shorts, and left her sherry glass in the sink. At the end of the hallway was Mary's closed door.

Dream on, sweetheart. By the time you get around to waking up, it will be too late.

She wondered what Mary would do. Would she kill herself? That might be kind of interesting.

17

WEDNESDAY WAS MARY's birthday. Fern had talked about it on Sunday. Mary thought she would remember it when the right day came, but Fern forgot.

Mary wanted to do something special. Something that she and the children would enjoy together, like the good times they had back home.

It was a hot day, and Cinni had taken them to the beach early. When they came back at noon, Mary asked, "Would you like to have lunch in the village today? Maybe at that little ice-cream parlor you wanted to try? Then afterward we can go and see the windmill Mrs. Reardon found for me, and the lighthouse, and. . . ."

They had just come in the door, and they stared at her without expression. In a moment of dizzying alarm, she felt as though they were not her children at all. Could she have made a mistake? They had Fern and Jason's faces, but the faces were somehow different. And they turned to Cinni. Waiting for their cue.

Cinni shrugged. "Don't count me in, okay? I'd just as soon stay here and work out on my surfboard. There are some nice waves today."

There could not have been good waves that day. It was a still, hot day.

Fern looked to her mother, then back at Cinni. Cinni shrugged again and smiled apologetically at Mary. "I hope you don't mind."

"No, that's quite all right." Mary was relieved that Cinni did not want to go. "All right, Fern and Jason, as soon as you wash off the salt and put on some halfway respectable clothes—"

Fern said, "I want to stay with Cinni."

"Me, too," added Jason.

"No, you have to go with Mom." Cinni dried a strand of hair with her towel. "It's your Mom's birthday, remember? How would you like it if she went surfing on *your* birthday?"

"But I want to go surfing." Fern seemed to pick up and echo Cinni's words.

Cinni glared at both children. "I told you, no." Her voice was low but firm.

They groaned. She said, "You're a couple of nasty little kids, treating your Mom this way. You'd better watch out, or Mom won't like you."

"Cinni—" Mary tried to stop her.

Cinni glanced at Mary with an ingratiating smile, as if to ask, I *am* doing all right, aren't I?

Mary bit her lip.

Fern began again. "But I wanna stay—"

"You're coming with me." Mary spoke sharply. "Poor Cinni's been on duty twenty-four hours a day since she came here. She deserves a little time to herself."

Fern burst out, "Aw, *shit!*" Mary was startled and alarmed. She had never heard Fern talk that way before. Some kids at the beach, perhaps?

She steered both children to the bathroom. Placing Jason, who was slightly more unresisting than his sister, in the tub, she went to find the clothes she thought they should wear.

Cinni came down the hall to her own room. "I'm sorry it turned out this way, Mrs. Shelburne. I tried—"

"I know, Cinni. It's all right."

It was not all right. Nothing was all right. She couldn't take the children against their will, not to a thing like that. She had already spoiled it for them and for herself. Anger had made her hasty.

And the girl—she had tried, she said? She had tried all the wrong things. How could such a bright girl have so little sense?

She reminded herself that Cinni was only fourteen. Oh, hell. Happy birthday, Mary. No ice cream today. No children.

She put away the clothes she had selected and got out their sunsuits instead. They could eat beans for lunch and then go back to the damn beach if they wanted to. With Cinni.

18

MARTINA SHELBURNE'S HOME base was the old family house in Shaker Heights. From there she circulated annually to Greece, where the cost of living was reasonable; to Morocco, for a week or two; to Ireland, for the scenery; a weekend in Paris—no explanation needed, as she pointed out; and always to the artists' colony at San Miguel de Allende, where she painted. For the remaining months, she visited her children in various parts of the country. She spent very little time in Shaker Heights.

She had opened her suitcase on the sofa and was unfolding two woolen shawls from Greece, rough textured things that shepherds might wear. They were for Gavin and Mary, or for wall hangings.

Fingering the shawls, Mary was awed, as usual, by her mother-in-law's itinerary. "They look Mexican," she said.

"But I haven't *been* to Mexico yet, lovey. That's next month."

"Isn't it hot there in summer?"

"Oh—it's elevated."

Would she go home to Shaker Heights before Mexico? Or would she stay in Mattapogue for a month? *Where* would she stay in Mattapogue for a month?

Fern held up a baby-faced doll in the dress of a Greek palace guard. "Look what Martina gave me. Mommy, why does he have a ballet costume?"

"It's traditional," said Mary. "Do they still have palace guards, Martina? Even if they don't have a—palace?"

"Of course they have palace guards," Martina replied. "Where would they be without palace guards? And look what I brought for you, dear."

Reaching into her bag again, she peeled away a layer of underwear and lifted out two bundles of brown paper.

Mary unwrapped the flat bundle first. "Oh, gorgeous! Martina, thank you!"

It was a brass tray with an intricate design pounded into it. The other bundle was a brass pitcher with a long, graceful spout.

"From Turkey," Martina said proudly. "You see, I always remember your birthday, don't I?"

"You certainly do. With a beautiful splash. Imagine lugging these things around in your suitcase."

Martina fluttered modestly. She was accustomed to lugging things around in her suitcase. She loved it. Cinni stood nearby, fingering a cheap Moroccan bracelet over which she had gushed, exclaiming that it was darling of Martina to think of her.

Martina snapped the suitcase closed. "Well, my dears, after all that trekking, I am a bit weary. Where are you putting me?"

"In my room," said Cinni. "I'll show you." She picked up the suitcase and led Martina down the hall. Cinni had moved her things into the room already shared by Fern and Jason. She had intended to sleep on an air mattress, or on the floor, or in sackcloth and ashes, but the Reardons had provided a folding cot. The room was wall-to-wall beds. Fern and Jason were thrilled, and Cinni was "glad to do it."

Mary followed them. After all, she, not Cinni, was the hostess.

"Dear," Martina was telling the girl, "I have some little medicines which the children ought to stay out of. I'm only telling you so you can keep an eye on them. I'll put them in the top drawer here—no, maybe I'd better keep them locked in the suitcase. It's sleeping pills and some other things. You know how foolish children are."

Cinni chuckled knowingly. She deposited the suitcase where Martina directed, fluffed up the pillow (unnecessarily), and departed, leaving Martina to stretch out on the bed with a huge sigh.

Mary asked, "Can I get you anything, Martina?"

"Nothing, dear. That girl of yours is a real treasure. I'm just enchanted with her."

Mary muttered grimly, "So is Gavin, I'm afraid."

Martina sat up. "Mary! What's gotten into you? For heaven's sake, we're talking about a *child*, and hardly a knockout, at that. This makes me worry about you. It must be the isolation out here, gives you too much time to reflect."

"Could be," said Mary reluctantly. She was hardly in a position to argue about a thing like that. It was only a feeling anyway, and perhaps it was due to boredom. Although, with her rich interior life, she was never consciously bored.

"Have a nice rest, Martina," she said, and withdrew.

Martina rested for two minutes, then followed her to the kitchen and mixed herself a daiquiri. "Where did the children disappear to?"

"Probably out with Cinni someplace. That's what I should have said, the children and Gavin are enchanted by her. To an almost unhealthy degree. I was, at first, but I'm less so now."

She had not meant to admit that. She had not meant to discuss Cinni at all any more. No one else would be able to see the situation as she saw it.

Martina apparently chose to take her remark lightly. "Well," she said with a little laugh, "I wish I had her charm."

"You certainly have, Martina. You have more than her charm."

"Thank you, dear. Can I make you a daiquiri?"

"I'd appreciate it."

A few minutes later, having drunk her daiquiri with

undue speed, Mary went looking for the children. She found them around at the side of the house, crouched in a circle of three below her bedroom window. She heard their voices as she approached, but they were suddenly silent, all watching her at once.

"What on earth are you doing here?" she asked.

"Playing a game," said Fern.

It had happened before, more than once; the abrupt silences, the looks that closed her out.

"Lunch is ready."

"We're busy," Fern replied.

Mary spoke sharply. "You can play the game later. But lunch is ready now and your grandmother is visiting, so don't get funny."

And then the sugared voice of Cinni. "Come on, angel. You don't want to let your mommy down when Grandma's visiting." She stood up and brushed the sand from her shorts.

"Mommy, you're always interrupting," Fern complained.

"That's life," said Mary.

She walked behind them, watching Cinni's back. The girl was either very gauche, or very, very clever.

She watched the girl closely when Gavin arrived the next evening, to see how they would behave with each other.

Maybe I'm crazy, she thought. But it can't be all in my mind.

Gavin's attention was focused on his mother. Yet over her shoulder, his eyes found Cinni. Cinni answered with a bland, noncommittal smile. Then he glanced at Mary, and she knew that Cinni, if not Gavin, was aware of being observed. The bland smile had been a warning.

She does know what she's doing.

Mary felt a moment of panic. To fight—this?

But how was Cinni doing it? Why would she want to?

Cinni stayed in the background for the rest of that

evening and the next day. The stage was Martina's and she used it to the fullest, telling them story after story of her travels.

There was plenty of time, Mary supposed. The whole rest of the summer. Cinni could afford the background for a while.

But she was never anywhere else. Never obtrusive, but always quiet and compliant. And yet she managed.

They planned a small party for Saturday night. Martina wanted to entertain her darling friends the Fowlers. Mary invited Esther and Jack Reardon.

It was an after-dinner party, with drinks, canapés, coffee, and cake. Mary wore a long dress in a bold Hawaiian print with a halter top. When she entered the living room before the guests arrived, Cinni exclaimed, "What a beautiful dress, Mrs. Shelburne. Do you have some sort of lacy stole you could wear over your shoulders?"

"No, I haven't," Mary replied. "Why, are we expecting a cold wave?"

"No, I just thought—"

"You thought my bones stick out, is that it?" Mary tried to sound pleasant. She had a weapon now. She had awareness.

"Well, you're a little thin on top." Cinni's eyes shifted to below the top. "And, um—that's not a maternity dress, is it?"

"No, it's not."

"It's kind of tight."

"Let's just say it's all wrong for me, okay?" Mary sailed into the kitchen, her heart beating fast. She should not have talked that way. It sounded downright hostile. She would tip her hand.

I'm not bony, she thought angrily. I *am* pregnant, and I'm not trying to hide it.

To make amends, she asked, "Cinni, how would you like to come and help me with these things? I never used frozen canapés before."

Cinni came cheerfully. She, too, was unwilling to tip

her hand in this cold war. The only trouble was, she already had.

The Fowlers arrived first. As Mary and Martina greeted them, Cinni slipped away down the hall. Almost subliminally, Mary observed her go into the room which she had given to Martina. Rather nervy of her, Mary thought vaguely. But after all, it really was her room.

Gavin met the Reardons for the first time and found them to his liking. Esther wore her pink caftan with a old Tutankhamen pendant, and Mary was plunged into thoughts of Luxor. It occurred to her, as she busied herself with cheese puffs and salted nuts, that perhaps someday she would actually like to see those places.

The thought startled her, but why not? Why live on dreams? Maybe her dreams were better, but they were meaningless. Her whole life was a dream. Even her children had been a dream, and she constantly tried to fit the reality into the framework of fantasy.

And Cinni had moved into the vacuum.

She looked out through the serving window at Cinni, perched on the arm of the sofa, swinging her leg back and forth; then at Gavin, mixing the drinks; at Martina, regaling the Fowlers with an account of her harrowing trip through some Grecian isle on the back of a donkey.

"My dears, I swear that poor little beast was no bigger than a Saint Bernard. My feet actually touched the ground. I'm telling you, I felt so sorry for the animal that I got off and walked, and they yelled at me to get back on. If gas weren't so expensive there, maybe they could use jeeps."

"That would ruin it," said Claire.

And Gavin said, "Yes, picturesqueness is always at somebody's expense."

"Not in Switzerland," his mother told him. "I don't think there are any victims in Switzerland."

Mary's eyes began to close. She set down her empty glass and considered a cup of instant coffee. She ought to have had some No-Doz on hand for times like this.

The fatigue, the urge to sleep, oozed through her body. She fought against it. It was as though her eyelids were weighted. She stopped listening to Martina's monologue, animated though it may have been. Retreating to the sink, she splashed cold water on her face and neck, even as soft cotton wool wrapped itself around her brain.

Cinni materialized beside her. "Are you all right, Mrs. Shelburne?"

"I'm desperately sleepy," Mary said. "I always get sleepy when I'm pregnant, but this is terrible."

"Maybe you ought to lie down for a while."

"I'd try coffee, but it never works fast enough. What am I going to do?"

"Come on, I'll help you lie down." Cinni led her back through the living room. Mary heard the stir of people jumping up to flock around her, saw a confusion of faces—Esther, floating in pink and gold, looking concerned, Martina muttering about calling a doctor.

"It's all right," said Mary, forcing her tongue to move. "I'm just suddenly very tired. I'm really thorry."

And Claire's voice following her down the hall. "Will somebody tell me what *happened?*"

Mary wanted to explain to them that she had only had one drink, that it was not what it seemed like. But talking was too much trouble. Beside her, Cinni murmured, "Just lie down for a little while. . . ."

" 'S torture," said Mary.

"I know. It happens to me sometimes, too. I just can't keep awake. It's very embarrassing."

"Mmmm." Mary sank down onto her bed. She wanted to die. Conking out so early in the evening, and at her own party. . . .

Maybe she would die. It was closing over her like water. She heard the click of the door. Forcing open her eyes, somehow moving her arm, she turned the lighted dial of the clock so that it faced her. She could always wake herself at any time she chose, as long as the clock faced her. Just five minutes. To take the edge off her sleepiness.

An hour later, the Reardons went home. Martina said, "Must you?" but they had finished their cake and coffee, and the whole thing didn't seem right without Mary.

When they had gone, Cinni murmured to Gavin, "I hope you don't mind, but I've just got to get outside and breathe some air." She glanced at the Fowlers, who were both smoking. The room was bathed in blue fog.

"I've half a mind to join you," Gavin said.

"Why don't you?"

"We'll see."

Cinni glanced back at him as she pushed open the door. Then she was gone. He hovered on the periphery, listening to his mother and the Fowlers talk about their far-flung adventures. It definitely was a periphery. He had not been to any of those places, and was not interested.

He coughed. The smoke was getting to him, too. He wandered about the room, watching to see if anybody noticed that he was drifting away. Nobody noticed.

It wasn't as if the host was walking out on his guests. With only the Fowlers there, Martina was more of a host than he was. They didn't care about him. He opened the screen door and stepped outside. He looked back just once more. They still didn't care.

Where was she? He peered around the corner of the house. She had meant it, hadn't she? He could not be mistaken about a thing like that.

He walked toward the beach, and as his head began to clear from three gins and tonics, he thought what a jackass he was being. An invitation from a fourteen-year-old girl? Hang on there, stupid, you could end up in prison. It made no difference what *she* wanted. It could even be a trap of some kind. Girls had been known to do that.

A flush of horrid realization fell over him as he remembered what had happened last week. God, would she hold that against him if things didn't go her way?

Maybe she wanted a raise. Maybe she was a juvenile blackmailer, who could tell?

He started back to the house.

From somewhere in the shadows came a whispered "Hi!"

He answered in his normal, employer tone of voice. "Is that you, Cinni?"

A soft giggle. "Who'd you think it was?"

"Good, I'm glad you didn't get mugged, or anything."

Another giggle. "Get mugged in a place like this? Gavin, rich people play other kinds of games."

"Do they, now?"

"For higher stakes."

She was standing beside him, her hands clasped behind her back in a childish fashion that thrust her breasts forward.

"Want to take a walk?" she asked.

"I just did take a walk."

"It's too nice a night to go back with all that smoke."

She had a point about the smoke. Just the same, he felt it was all a ploy to get him where she wanted him. Wherever that was.

He put his arm around her waist. "Listen, Cinni, you just said rich people have games. Poor people have games, if you call mugging a game. What's *your* game?"

She became a bundle of indignation, drawing back and detaching his arm from her middle. "What do you mean?"

"I could get in a lot of trouble."

She must know it already. He was not jeopardizing anything to remind her of the fact.

"Do you want me to get in a lot of trouble?" he asked.

Her face loomed close to his, an upturned moon. "Who's going to know?" she whispered. "*I* wouldn't tell. Don't you trust me, Gavin?"

He put his hand under her chin. "In the adult world, my dear, and especially in the business world, you learn not to trust anybody. Not a soul. Without being hostile or paranoid, you just never give them the benefit of the doubt in a risky situation."

She removed his hand from her face. She was always removing his hand, as if he was pawing her. But he was only being fatherly, hoping to put her off. She melted into him. The top of her head came almost to his mouth, all that warm golden hair. She stood on tiptoe and thrust herself against him.

"I could make it real nice for you, Gavin."

He asked gently, "What the hell does a kid your age know about making things real nice?"

"A lot. Didn't I prove it before?"

He would have to terminate this ludicrous situation, and fast. But not make her angry. Who knew what she might do?

She began grinding against him. It hit him like a shock wave.

"Cynthia, you're a dear." Hell, he was starting to sweat. He tried to pull away from her, but she came with him.

"You're a darling, Cynthia, but not now."

"Why not now? You're ready and I'm ready."

He suddenly became aware that they might not be just two figures on the beach. "Cynthia, people can see us."

"Oh, we wouldn't do it here. What do you think?"

"I know that, but—wait a minute." He eased her away.

"You're just trying to get rid of me."

"For now, yes. But maybe—"

"What's wrong with now? She's asleep. And I saw the Fowlers going home a while ago, and—"

"And my mother will stay up having another diaquiri, and she'll see us come in together. . . ."

"We don't have to go in together."

She had an answer for everything, the brat. She was bound to get him in trouble. Martina was much too sophisticated not to start adding things up in her little mind. It might already be too late.

"Next week?" he suggested desperately. "This is just not a good time."

"A *week!* I might be having my period."

"Ssh. Quiet. Do as I say. I'm older and wiser. You go in first, and I'll follow."

When they reached the house, she stood on her toes and looked in a window.

"Gavin, there's nobody in the living room."

"Go ahead in."

She went in. How long should he wait? Actually, it was pretty artificial. If he came in on her heels, whatever the interval, it would look suspicious, but he was damned if he'd hang around for twenty minutes, feeling like an idiot. When he was sure she was out of the way, he strode up to the door and pulled it open.

She was standing in the living room, her hands in the pockets of her blue sundress. She had come face to face, as it were, with Mary, who had put on her nightgown and was just leaving the kitchen with a cup of something that steamed.

To his relief, Cinni had it all under control. "Are you feeling better, Mrs. Shelburne?"

Mary looked as if she was going to speak, but she didn't. Her cool eyes ran up and down Cinni, then up and down Gavin, and then she walked away toward the bedroom with her coffee.

Jesus.

Cinni turned to him and shrugged. "Play it cool," she advised.

He felt a surge of anger. It was easy to be angry with her, but he was the one who had taken her up on her obvious invitation and followed her outside. Where was his usually sharp mind?

He started picking up dirty cups and cake plates. "You go on to bed," he said.

"There's somebody in the bathroom."

Martina. Hell. He felt as if the two women were aligned against him.

"Okay, then, help me with the dishes."

19

MARY WOKE IN the morning, hearing the door to her room softly close. For a moment she thought it was still night, and someone was coming in, and she would have to go back to the party. It was the last thing she wanted to do.

The children were up, she could hear their voices. And the person who had come into the room was Gavin. He wore his bathrobe and smelled of shaving lotion.

"Time to get up," he greeted her cheerily.

She groaned. "Not for me, I feel rotten."

"What's the matter?"

"If you want to know, I've felt rotten since last night. And all I had was one little drink."

"Maybe it's the pregnancy."

"I can drink even when I'm pregnant, and not conk out like that. I think—"

She did not want to tell him what she thought. He would laugh at her. But she remembered Martina's sleeping pills, and Cinni disappearing into that room. She closed her eyes and felt sick, and thanked God she was not dead.

But the baby—My God, the baby. What if it were brain-damaged?

Even if it were, she would have no proof of what had happened. Only her surmise, which she knew was correct.

My baby . . . A tear squeezed from her closed eyes.

"Is it that bad?" Gavin asked in alarm. "Maybe we should get a doctor."

"I don't need a doctor."

If the baby were injured, it was already too late.

"Martina woke me last night," she said, "so I could wash and go to bed properly. I felt so groggy I thought I was going to die. I went out to the kitchen and made some coffee. It's supposed to clear your head."

"Nothing really clears your head." He took off his robe and began to dress. "You have to wait till the alcohol leaves your system."

"Not that. Not alcohol."

She waited for him to ask what she meant. He did not seem to notice that there was anything to ask. He put on his bathing trunks, his tennis shirt, and a pair of khaki slacks over the trunks. He was getting ready to swim. To enjoy his summer. She loved him so much. All this other, this horror—if she could tear it up by the roots and burn it, then their lives would be good once more.

But perhaps she could not accomplish it in time. She would lose them all first, Gavin and Fern and Jason. She would be left alone with Christopher. Or Daphne. And the baby might be brain-damaged.

"Can I bring you anything?" he asked.

"No, I'm getting up."

Later, when they were gathering for breakfast, Martina appeared, elegantly attired in a white pantsuit. "Well, ladies and gentlemen, I think I'll take my leave tonight."

Mary cried, "Tonight? Oh, Martina!"

"Time to check in on old Shaker Heights, and then off to Mexico. I'll take the train in with Gavin, spend the night, and catch a morning plane."

She had it all settled. Undoubtedly the little house was too crowded for comfort. But Mary dreaded being alone again with Cinni.

She could have killed me, Mary thought, *with that sleeping pill and the alcohol.*

She hoped Martina would not be able to get a reservation.

It turned out Martina already had a reservation. Everything seemed preordained. Even being alone with Cinni.

Mary put through a call to Dr. Tucker to ask about any danger to the baby. It would be nice, she thought, if Cinni were to overhear her, and know that she had been found out. But when Dr. Tucker returned the call, after the answering service had spent an hour tracking her down, no one was in the living room.

The baby was probably all right, she assured Mary. It would not have affected the oxygen supply.

"If I died, it might have," Mary replied. She was disappointed in Dr. Tucker's lack of alarm over what had happened. Probably the doctor did not even believe her.

They were getting ready for the beach, and Mary was filling a half-gallon thermos with cold water and ice cubes for the children, when Gavin came into the kitchen. She ignored him. She had been cool to him all during breakfast. She hoped Martina would not notice, but couldn't help it if she did. She simply could not bring herself to be friendly after last night.

"Look," he said. "Something's bugging you."

Really. She did not need him to tell her that.

"I've been trying to figure out what it is," he continued. The old smoothie. "And all I can think of is when you saw me come in last night."

That proved it. If he were truly innocent, he would not even have thought of it.

Still she said nothing. He grew uncharacteristically flustered. "I could tell by the way you looked at us—at me. And I want you to stop and think. You know me better than that."

"Better than what?" She stared at him blankly.

"Better than to think—" He couldn't say it.

"Think what?"

"Whatever you were thinking."

"What was I thinking?"

"*You* know." He sounded like Jason.

He had really gotten himself out on a limb. She almost enjoyed it. She closed the cap on the thermos jug and started out to the beach. The others had already left.

He sprinted past her and blocked her access to the front door. "Wait, Mary, I want to get this straightened out."

She could have gone out through the kitchen, but then he would have sprinted again. It might have been quite funny, their tearing back and forth all morning. She could have used a good laugh, but not the exercise. She stood before him, clasping the jug. It was pleasantly cool.

"Gavin, if you have something on your mind that you would like to talk about, why don't you just get it over with? This is ridiculous."

"I only want to tell you, it's not what you think."

She had the sensation of having gone around in a circle.

"I went outside to clear my head," he told her. "After a couple of drinks—you know. The girl went out, too, about the same time, to see the moonlight on the water."

"Moonlight was on the water?"

"There *was* moonlight on the water." He sounded as if he was trying to reassure himself about the moonlight on the water. "Not the best, of course, since it wasn't exactly a full moon."

"I can imagine. Gavin, this jug is rather heavy. May we proceed to the beach?"

He leaped to take it from her, and held the door open so they could both go out.

"I think it was all a big mistake," she said as they walked together.

He looked alarmed. "What?"

"My hiring that girl. I don't really need her. I thought I would. I thought I'd like the companionship as well as the help, but she's more trouble than she's worth. Why don't you take her back with you?"

"What do you mean, trouble? What trouble?"

"A problem of interpersonal relations. I find it very tiring."

"Do you mean you don't get along with her?"

"On the surface I suppose you might say we get along, but there's more to it than meets the eye. I really don't think I should have to explain further."

"Mary, I thought I told you—"

"It doesn't matter what you told me, Gavin, I want that girl out. Before something happens. Do you understand? No, you wouldn't. But she was hired to help me, and since she's doing the opposite, she's got to go. I wish you understood."

They had almost reached the little group on the beach. Gavin muttered, "You can't fire a girl with no notice."

The beach, although wide open under a sultry yellow sky, seemed airless. Cinni had put up the umbrella, but lay beyond its shade. She wore a black bikini and had oiled her brown-gold skin to a high gloss. It was a fanatical dedication to tanning that amounted almost to self-punishment under that suffocating sunshine.

Mary huddled in the shade of the umbrella with Martina and Jason. Martina, in a green swimdress and huge violet goggles, inched over to her and put an oily hand on Mary's arm. "I hate to leave you people, but the schedule says move on. Watch that baggage, will you?" She jerked her chin toward Cinni. "I wouldn't trust her around my home."

A shaft of joy leaped and shimmered, and Mary squeezed the hand that held her arm.

"So you noticed."

"I could hardly help noticing. It's disgusting, a child her age. I wonder if her mother knows."

"Quite possibly they're two of a kind," said Mary. She hoped that she and Martina were talking about the same thing.

Cinni raised her head and rolled over onto her side. "Oh-h-h, hot." She sat up. "Anybody going in the water?"

"I'm digging," said Fern.

"What are you making?"

"A tunnel."

"It's going to collapse in the middle."

Fern looked up, nonplussed, but Cinni's eyes were already roaming the next generation, and the next. "Aren't you people hot?"

"Oh, definitely," said Martina.

Only Gavin ignored her. Cinni walked over to where he sat and poured a handful of sand onto his back. It stuck in the rivulets of sweat.

"Now you'll have to wash it off." She turned and skittered into the water, kicking up a small spray of sand.

Gavin reached up awkwardly and tried to brush his back.

"Go on, Gavin, wash it off," said Mary.

With icy reproach, his eyes met hers. He got up and waded into the water. Mary could feel Martina waiting to exchange looks. She did not oblige, but concentrated on her towel, brushing away each grain of sand that Cinni had kicked there.

Far out in the water, Gavin swam strongly. The double overarm was the only stroke he knew, but he did it well. He had left Cinni bobbing in the waves near the shore, watching hm.

Fern, with a large soup spoon, was trying to deepen her tunnel so it would not collapse. "Martina, Cinni's got a surfboard."

"Yes, I saw it," her grandmother replied.

"Do you know how to surf?"

"Absolutely not. You wouldn't catch *me*."

"Daddy can do it. Daddy's even better than Cinni."

"If you ask me," said Mary, "Cinni oughtn't to be surfing until she gets better at swimming."

Still in the same spot, Cinni jumped, rising with each swell, then settling back on her feet, the troughs of water tickling her rump.

"She can swim real good," Fern said indignantly. "She just doesn't want to, right now."

"Oh, is that what she tells you? Is that why she nearly drowned her first day here?"

"Well, she can swim. You can't surf unless you can swim."

Mary was glad that Fern knew that. At least she wouldn't try anything foolish.

Cinni bobbed, still watching Gavin, and Gavin still swam, arm over arm. Martina stood up and went to splash herself with water. Hesitantly she waded in, swam a few strokes, and came back.

"It is co-o-old." She began to rave about Greece. Mary imagined her paddling about with a snorkel and fins, scooping up sponges.

Gavin was coming in now. She saw him catch a wave and ride it toward the shore. Cinni followed him up the slope of the beach. "Gavin, that was terrific. That was really body surfing. I didn't know you could do it."

Gavin's face remained a stone mask. He barely acknowledged Cinni's praise as he toweled his face and hair. Was he honestly in a rotten mood? Mary wondered. Or just trying to throw his wife off the scent?

Martina went back to the house to finish packing. Later that day, Mary at last had her picnic at Montauk Point, because Martina thought it would be fun. Cinni went with them, by now ignoring Gavin as completely as he seemed to be ignoring her. The children, however, were her slaves. They followed her everywhere, into the pine woods, down to the beach, and they refused to walk over to the lighthouse because Cinni did not care to see it up close.

Mary watched, and wondered what she could possibly want with them. A young girl should be living a life of her own.

A life of her own, she reflected. Cinni's trying to live *my* life.

20

THE SUN WAS a red ball in the sky when Mary drove home from the station. In the rear-view mirror she could see Cinni in the back seat with a child snuggled on either side of her. It made Mary feel like an outsider to have them all in back, away from her, but that was only secondary to the hurt of Gavin's chilly behavior. He had not kissed her or even told her goodbye. From time to time her anger would burn brightly, and she would think: How dare he? I wasn't the one who did anything wrong.

And then the pain would subside to a dull ache. She tried to tell herself once more that it was only guilt on his part, and guilt often made people angry. But she could not help wondering if he might really be drawing away from her.

When they reached the house, and it was time for the children to go to bed, she was reminded of last week. It was that same time a week ago, when the two of them were alone together, that Cinni had told her about Gavin.

Mary had been so embarrassed. She remembered the way she had cringed inside.

And this week, had Cinni been more willing? She certainly had not been less willing. Mary had seen their faces.

"Leave the dishes," she said, knowing Cinni would wash them anyway. "I'm going to bed."

"Aren't you feeling well, Mrs. Shelburne?"

"Just tired." Mary gritted her teeth. Everything about the girl was false, even her concern.

Get out of here. Got to get her out of here, she thought later as she lay in bed, listening to the surf.

On what grounds? Can you tell a girl she is destroying your family, when she already knows it?

What am I going to do?

After some time, although she did not know how, the sound of the surf lulled her to sleep. It was a poor sleep, a confusion of dreams. No solution came to her in the night, as she had hoped it would. She still did not know what to tell the girl.

In the morning she rose early, largely because she could not sleep any more. The three of them were all together at breakfast, as they were every morning.

The three children. Cinni, too, was a child.

A *child.*

What am I going to do? Mary wondered again.

She had to wait until the children went out to play. It took them a while. It almost seemed as though Cinni was trying to keep them with her.

As Mary had known she would, Cinni had washed the dinner dishes. She would have to praise her for it.

She heard Cinni call, "I'll be ready for the beach in a minute, Fernie. You just wait there."

Mary raised her voice. "It's only eight o'clock." She stood in the kitchen, emboldening herself with coffee.

Cinni appeared in the doorway. "I thought we'd go early, before it gets too hot. It's going to be another day like yesterday."

Another yellow sky? Mary looked out of the window. It was a high overcast of bright white clouds.

"Cinni, I appreciate your doing the dishes, but you didn't have to."

Cinni, who had started toward her room to change for the beach, turned back.

"Oh, that's okay, Mrs. Shelburne. How are you feeling?"

"Nothing wrong. I was just tired. I wear out easily when I'm pregnant."

No reason to fire the girl. Yet she had to do it. This could not go on.

"Cinni, I'd like to talk to you."

Again the girl turned back. "Yes, Mrs. Shelburne?"

Mary invited her to sit down. It made it easier, with Mary standing. Cinni pulled out a chair and sat at the kitchen table. Mary leaned against the counter, holding her coffee cup in her hand.

"Cinni, last spring when we talked about this job, I was in danger of losing my baby. I thought I'd need some extra help, so I wouldn't get overly tired. That was my doctor's advice. But now, everything seems fine. I don't think the problem is there any more."

"Did the doctor say it's okay?" Cinni asked eagerly.

"Of course."

The doctor had, although not in so many words, when Mary saw her in June. But by then the commitment was made.

She did not know how to go on from there.

She closed her eyes, and opened them again. Cinni watched her calmly. "Is that what you wanted to tell me, Mrs. Shelburne? I'm glad for you."

Mary set down her cup. She felt ridiculous holding it.

"What I'm trying to say is, I don't feel this is working out very well, and since I no longer need the extra help, I think we'd better terminate the whole arrangement."

"What arrangement?"

Damn.

"Cinni, in other words, I'm trying to tell you that your services will no longer be needed."

"Why?"

"Because, as I said, this hasn't been working out the way I'd hoped."

"Why? What did you hope?"

"I'd hoped—for a slightly different pattern of interpersonal relations."

Damn, that phrase again. She had counted on the right words coming when she needed them.

"I don't understand, Mrs. Shelburne. What did I do wrong?"

"Cinni, it's a very involved situation, as I'm sure you realize, and I think it's time to end it."

"But what did I do?"

What did you do? You tried to take away my husband and my children, but I'm not going to mention it. You'd have an answer for that, too.

"What did I do, Mrs. Shelburne?"

"As I said, it just isn't working out. And this is my decision."

"What's your decision?"

"*To terminate this arrangement.*"

"I don't understand, Mrs. Shelburne."

"Cinni, I don't think I could make it any plainer. I know you've enjoyed being here, and having the beach, and it's probably too late for you to find another job, but I feel I'm doing the right thing for all of us."

She turned away and began wiping the counter. The conversation was over. She had made her point.

"Do you mean you're sending me home, Mrs. Shelburne?"

"I'm afraid so. You can have your morning at the beach, and then take a train this afternoon. Would you like to call your mother and tell her you're coming?"

She heard a sharp intake of breath.

"You wouldn't send me home. What would I tell her? I don't want to go home. I was so glad to get out of there and come here, and be with you people. . . ."

That's me, thought Mary. *She's me.* The child who had once appealed to her, the younger version of herself, had suddenly reappeared. Her heart opened and bled a little, but only for a moment.

God, but she's slippery.

"I'm terribly sorry, Cinni, but I am not running a shelter for girls who don't get along with their mothers. You'll receive severance pay, of course. I'll give you quite a generous settlement, because I know this is rather sudden."

"It's *very* sudden, and I still don't know what I did. Would you please just explain to me what I did?"

"As I *said*—" Again Mary's jaw tightened, making her voice shrill.

Cinni picked it up from there. "You said the arrangement is not working out. But *how* is it not working out? I'm sorry, but I can't accept that as an explanation, because it doesn't tell me anything."

"I'm afraid you'll have to accept it. I'm the employer here. As I said, you'll get a very nice severance pay."

Mary's head began to reel and her breathing came hard. She had never expected this.

"So, my dear," she continued, trying with a patronizing attitude to maintain the upper hand, "from now, I'm taking over as mother." She started toward the back door, only to discover that Fern and Jason were on the other side of it, peering in and listening.

"Time to get ready for the beach," she told them.

Fern opened the door and came in slowly, with Jason following. "What happened? I heard somebody shouting."

No one had shouted, but Fern did not know how to describe what she had heard.

"We're going to the beach, is what happened," Mary said.

Fern narrowed her eyes. "With you?"

"With me. I'm your mother, remember?"

"Why can't we go with Cinni?" The child's question was a bewildered wail. She had heard too much.

"Cinni can come, too, if she wants to. Then in the afternoon, we'll take her to the station."

"I want Cinni!"

Cinni stepped forward and drew the girl close to her. "You have me, Fern honey."

"Fern and Jason, get ready for the beach." Mary

spoke more harshly than she meant to. Her poise was snapping. She had failed. She could not get rid of the girl. In all her previous experience, when people were fired, dammit, they were fired. They left. They were never seen again.

"Cinni, you're only making it more difficult for yourself and for them."

Good. She could still hang on. She was the adult here. Her word was law.

"They don't want me to go, Mrs. Shelburne."

"They'll get over it, and so will you. Now go to your room, Fern, and put on your bathing suit. You, too, Jason."

"No," said Fern. "I want to stay with Cinni."

Mary seized the child's arm and pulled her sharply away from Cinni. "*Go*. Do as you're told." She pushed Fern in the direction of her room and gave Jason a little spank.

The children began to cry.

"*Go!*" shouted Mary.

With howls and tears, the children fled.

Cinni stared at her, horror-stricken. "You didn't have to do that, Mrs. Shelburne."

"Obviously, I did have to." Mary was exhausted. Fern's arm had felt like a toothpick in her hand. How could she have come to this?

Feeling elephantine with her pregnancy, she followed the children and found them sitting on the floor of their room, crying.

"Mommy, you're so mean!" Fern wept.

"I'm sorry I had to be mean," Mary told her quietly. "But you know, you've gotten very fresh toward me lately. You've started to think that Cinni is your mother, not me, and that's not true. It's not right."

She stuffed them into their bathing suits and herded them, still sobbing, into the living room, to wait for her while she picked up the towels from the railing at the back steps. Her coffee still sat on the counter, by now cold. She needed it, and there was no time to make it fresh. She drank it quickly, gathering up the towels, her beach bag, and the children.

Cinni joined them, demure in her white bikini with the pink coin dots. She acted as though nothing had happened. How could she? Why can't I be cold-blooded like that? Mary wondered.

It was early, and very few people were on the beach. Mary set up the umbrella and spread out her towel. The sky was still white. It could become cloudy. It could even rain. She hoped it would rain. Somehow it was easier to accept change if the weather changed, too.

Fern asked, "Will you build a fort with us, Cinni?" Both she and Jason ignored Mary. They did not seem to know what to make of her.

Mary had brought a book and her sunglasses, but she could not read. Her head ached. She glanced at her watch. Nine o'clock. If they went back at eleven, it couldn't possibly take Cinni more than an hour to pack. Then they would eat a quick lunch and she could catch the one-forty train.

And then Cinni would be gone and life would return to normal. She would have her children again. They could do all the lovely things they always did together. Another visit to the cemetery, perhaps. And then the windmill. The children had not yet seen Esther's windmill. And the ice-cream parlor.

God, but she felt hung over. A stabbing headache, a bit of nausea, and she could not keep her eyes open.

The waves crashed rhythmically. There was no wind. The tide was either going out or coming in. How silly of her. Of course it was either going out or coming in. If she watched it for a while, she would know which, but it didn't really matter.

Her back began to hurt? Why didn't she have a backrest or a sand chair? She had not previously spent enough time on the beach to know she needed one.

To ease the discomfort, she lay down, curled on her side so she could watch the children while she listened to the surf. Her head pounded. She did not want to go into the house and take an aspirin. She did not want to leave them.

Cinni gave her a long, appraising stare.

She'll never know how rotten I feel, thought Mary. Not only physically, right now, but in general, too. About her. But she made me hate her. I just want her out.

Her eyes blinked closed. She forced them open. She felt so terrible, she might even die. If she could die like this, it would not be half bad, lying there listening to the waves washing near her feet.

21

MARY DID NOT know when she slept; was not aware that the confusion of dreams meant sleep. She was not aware of anything until she sat up suddenly, her feet cold and wet.

For a moment she stared at the receding water. Then she thought: so that's what it's doing, it's coming in. She looked over to where they were building the fort. They were not there. The fort had been washed away.

Another wave came at her, but did not quite reach her. She stood up to pull back her towel. The beach was still almost empty, yet it looked different, somehow. The arrangement of people was different. The pale sunshine was gone.

She squinted up at the sky. It was covered with low, gray clouds. A light wind had risen. Her watch said—

God, no! It was after two o'clock. She had slept for five hours. Why hadn't they waked her?

They had gone in for lunch, and they hadn't waked her. Five hours!

Damn me, she thought as she folded the umbrella and her towel. Five hours, in the daytime? It was impossible.

Not impossible to fall asleep when she was pregnant, but to sleep so soundly?

She thought they would be there when she reached the house. They would be playing out in back, or in their room. Playing Go Fish, or Old Maid. Fern had all the makings of a card shark.

Their sand toys were on the floor near the dining table: their little plastic buckets, and the kitchen spoons which she had bought for them when the plastic shovels broke. There was the sand mold in the shape of a green starfish, and one wet towel.

"Fern? Jason?"

She could not bring herself to call Cinni. She had fired the girl, but now it was too late to get her onto any sort of decent train that day. The trains did not run often on weekdays.

"Jason? Fern?"

Something had been wrong outside. She could not quite place it, with a brain still fuzzy from her long sleep. She went to the front door and looked out.

The car was gone.

The car can't have gone without me, she whispered to the door.

Her first thought was that someone had stolen it. But it seemed unlikely that anyone would take the trouble to walk all the way to this remote spot, down a quarter of a mile of sandy lane, to steal a five-year-old station wagon.

She turned from the door and searched through all the bedrooms, the bathroom. She looked out of all the windows, and she listened.

Cinni could not have driven the car away. Cinni was only fourteen, and fourteen-year-olds do not drive cars in New York State. It must have been that Gavin had come back.

Gavin had come back for some reason, she could not imagine why, and driven away with Cinni and the children.

Cinni was the reason. And Cinni wanted the children, too, so they had taken the children. They had taken everything—except Christopher, they could not take Christopher.

They've taken my whole life.

She sat down next to the telephone, in a corner of the

living room opposite the dining table. At first she could not remember his number. Her hand seemed to be made of rubber. She started to dial. Then she hung up, because she had not dialed the area code. Two-one-two. That was it. Two-one-two, and then his office number.

The company operator answered. Funny the way operators never quite sounded like people. Mary asked for his extension.

The phone buzzed in her ear. Gavin's secretary answered. She did not recognize Mary's voice and asked who was calling please.

"His wife. Is he there?"

"Just a moment, Mrs. Shelburne."

He would not be there, of course. He had come out on the train and driven away with Cinni and the children. What would they have done if Mary had not slept?

She remembered the coffee. . . .

"Yes, Mary, what's up?"

"You're there?"

"Of course I'm here. What's the matter?"

"They're gone. The children are gone. And Cinni and the car."

"Wait a minute. What?"

"They're *gone*," she repeated.

He was still being dense. She had to tell him the whole story of what had happened that morning, while precious time ticked by. Even then he missed the point.

"I don't know why you had to be so hasty and come down on the girl like that," he said. "She's only a kid. It's no wonder—"

"*Only a kid?*"

"Take it easy, will you? Nothing's going to happen. They'll come back."

"How do you know?"

"What else would they do? You're making it into an awful melodrama. I just hope she knows how to handle the car."

Mary's voice broke. "I told you yesterday to take her

back with you. Now she has the children, and God knows where they are. Gavin, she's dangerous! My coffee—My drink that night—"

"Now wait a minute, Mary. You're all wrought up."

"Of course I'm wrought up!" She slammed down the receiver. She knew it would not slam in his ear, it would only make the usual click of hanging up, but she could not put it down any other way.

Damn Gavin. Why must he stop and analyze her? That was scarcely the problem.

And her coffee. The drink, that night at Martina's party. He would never believe her. But she could not possibly have slept like that either time, despite being pregnant, all on her own. And Martina had told Cinni exactly where she kept her sleeping pills.

Stumbling in bare feet over stiff grass roots, she ran across the sand to the Reardons' house.

Thank God they were both there, round-faced Jack with his horn-rimmed glasses, Esther in pink shorts.

"Have you seen my children? And the babysitter? Our car? They're all gone. I fell asleep on the beach. Had trouble with the sitter—I fired her this morning. And they're all—No, wait. Did you happen to see the car drive away, and who was driving?"

Jack said, "No, we didn't. Not a thing."

"Do you need any help?" asked Esther.

Do I need any help, Mary repeated as she ran back to her own house.

The telephone again. She had to look up the number. She did not know how to call the police in a strange place.

It seemed to be 911 everywhere, for emergencies. She dialed 911.

"I want to report my children missing, and their babysitter. She's a fourteen-year-old girl with long blond hair. The children are a six-year-old girl, dark hair and green eyes, and a four-year-old boy with light brown hair. And they must have taken my car, because it's not here."

She could not give Jason's eye color. It was a mixture

of gray, green and blue, and she did not know what to call it.

She was proud of the way she had kept her head and described the children instead of screaming.

"This babysitter," the police said, "is she a member of your household? Has she used the car before?"

"She's only *fourteen*. Of course she hasn't used the car. And—you see, I just fired her. She must have taken them because I fired her."

"Where were you when this happened?"

She stared at the ceiling and gave a silent scream.

"I took the children to the beach—while the sitter was packing to leave." It sounded better than to say she had fired the sitter and then taken her to the beach.

"And I haven't been well. I fell asleep."

"Maybe one of the kids got hurt and she took 'em to a doctor."

"*Please* listen to me. It's not like that. Something happened. This girl is—she's not normal. That's why I fired her."

Why couldn't they understand? Why hadn't she known?

"Can you give the description of the car? License number?"

Fortunately she knew the license number. Some people don't know their own license numbers, she thought. She knew the make, the model, the year, and the color: dark blue. She had done her part. Now they would have to do theirs.

"You say the sitter was driving the car?" they asked. "Anybody see her?"

"No, but who else? My husband is in his office."

They did not ask her to explain that statement. She understood what they meant. It might have been a kidnapping.

"It is a kidnapping," she told them brokenly. "It is."

"We'll do everything we can, ma'am. We'll put out a description right away."

She hung up the telephone and walked to the front door. Nothing. She walked back again, the length of the living room. She walked and walked, because she could not sit still.

She had reached the door again, and opened it to look out, when the telephone rang.

She ran all the way back to it. It would be the police. They had found—

It was Gavin. "Any news yet?"

"No. They're gone. I called the police."

"Good God, Mary, aren't you overreacting? Why the police? She probably took them out to McDonald's, or something."

"For five hours?"

"Well . . ."

"I'm just waiting here," she told him pointlessly. "I can't *do* anything."

"Of course you can't do anything. You wait there by the telephone. That's the best thing you can do." And then it burst out of him with a vehemence that surprised her: "I wish you hadn't fired her."

Again, a silent scream at the ceiling. It could have been any one of those other bland, innocuous, perfectly bright but not so brilliant girls.

Instead, she had picked Cinni. For her maturity. What a joke. Cinni was precocious—maybe too precocious—but not mature.

"The Reardons didn't see anything," she said. "I asked."

"Keep me posted, okay? And stop worrying."

Any one of those girls. But how could she have guessed? How could she have seen the hunger?

Even after it started, she couldn't see the hunger. It simply did not show.

She began to walk again. To the door. And back. Gavin, sitting in his office. Keep me posted. Stop worrying.

A bump inside her abdomen. She bent over, hugging it fiercely. *This might be the only child I have left.*

How could he just sit there and sell plastic kitchenware?

He sat with his chair turned to the window and stared at the building across the street. He could see into a dentist's office. The dentist's chair faced the window. Those people had a lovely view of Gavin while their teeth were drilled and filled. He didn't suppose they spent much time looking at him. There was nothing to see. The woman there now, for instance, clutching her pocketbook under the white sheet, did she know she was looking at a man—

To hell with that woman. He ran a hand through his hair. Damn the whole mess. An hour's weakness, and here he was like a fly in a web. She'd talk. He knew she would.

How would they know who to believe? How did they ever know? He'd heard of teachers who got accused and then absolved. How did they prove it, one way or the other?

And it didn't make any difference about the girl. The one in the Roman Polanski case, from all reports, had been around before, but that didn't mitigate the circumstances. Except there the charge was rape. With Cinni, it wasn't rape.

But how would they know who to believe?

To the door again. She did not like that wind out there. As far as she knew, they were still in their bathing suits. Even a warm wind could feel chilly when there was no sun.

She huddled against the door frame. Worrying about whether they were cold. Were they even alive?

The phone!

She picked it up before it could ring again, bracing herself in case it was Gavin.

A low laugh came over the wire.

"You sound a little upset, Mrs. Shelburne, I wonder

why. Too bad I couldn't reach you sooner. You've been tying up the phone."

"Cinni—"

"Don't keep me talking, you bitch. I've got the kids, as you probably guessed, and you know why. Just for your information, I could have had him, too. You know that, don't you? I could have him any time, and it scares the shit out of you, right?"

Then Mary was listening to the terrible hum of a disconnected line.

Cinni had not even said what to do to get them back.

She doesn't mean to give them back. Not ever.

Mary waited a few minutes, in case Cinni should call again. She had hung up quickly, of course, so the call could not be traced. Clever child. But she might have meant to say more.

The phone was silent. She rested her hand on it, willing it to ring. Then she picked it up and dialed Gavin's office.

"He's just gone out, Mrs. Shelburne," his secretary reported. "He didn't say when he'd be back. I'll tell him you called."

Mary dropped the phone into place. It wasn't the secretary's fault. She tensed her hands into claws, buried her face in them, and screamed.

The scream died away. She ran into Cinni's room and began pulling out drawers. Where were those sleeping pills? Where? She needed to know.

Bikinis, shorts, underpants were all over the floor when Esther Reardon appeared in the doorway.

Esther had changed her clothes. Instead of the pink shorts, she now wore a chino skirt. She took a step into the room. "Mary." She held out her arms. "Is there anything we can do?"

"Oh, God," said Mary. "Just find my children."

"I wish I'd seen something," Esther said.

"It doesn't matter now. She called me. She has them. Revenge, I suppose. She's in love with Gavin."

"Oh, no. That *child?*"

"People make jokes," said Mary, "about dogs and cats that don't know they're dogs and cats. Esther, she doesn't know she's a child."

Mary pulled a suitcase out from under the bed. It was empty. She felt in one of the side pockets. A round plastic box. Eagerly she pulled it out. Inside the box was a dial, each hole filled with a yellow tablet set in cellophane. Only one compartment was empty.

"I see what you mean," said Esther.

Mary closed the box. "How can a girl that age get a prescription?"

"Some doctors, some parents, think it's better than getting pregnant."

"I was looking for sleeping pills. She stole some from Martina and used them on me twice. Once was the party. I didn't know then. The other was today."

"Do you have proof?"

"That's what I'm looking for. It doesn't matter. I just wanted something to do."

It had seemed to matter once. Esther helped her up from the floor and they went into the living room. Jack Reardon stood at the front door, watching the road. He turned when they came in.

"Took us a little while," he told Mary, removing a cold pipe from his mouth. "I guess the thing didn't quite register at first. Then we got to talking about it."

Mary shrugged. "There's not much anybody can do, except talk." She felt a quiet death inside her. But it would break again. Suddenly it would tell her *Fern and Jason are gone*, and then she would fall apart.

"What am I going to do?" she asked.

Her eyes lit on the telephone. "I didn't tell them about her call!"

She dialed the police again. She had not thought to ask them for a more direct number than 911.

She identified herself, reminded them of what had happened. They had not forgotten.

"I heard from the girl. She called me a little while ago. She took the children in revenge."

"Did she say anything—"

"Nothing. Nothing about giving them back. I don't know where they are. I don't believe this, you know."

They spoke soothingly. "We're working on it, Mrs. Shelburne. We put out a bulletin on the car."

"Can't you *do* something?"

"Believe me, I know how you feel. We are doing something. It's only a matter of time."

"Then why can't you find it?"

She had to keep them talking. Once the connection was broken, she would be helpless again.

"I don't see why you can't find the car. It must be on the road somewhere, and it's a pretty big car." She repeated the license number, the color, the make, the year—

"We have all that, Mrs. Shelburne. Now please try to stay calm."

Esther stood beside her, listening. Mary knew she had cracked too far. They would think she was insane.

She hung up the phone. "I can't stand it," she explained, "just sitting here."

Esther put an arm around her. "I know. I feel the same way."

It's not your children, Mary thought. She could not imagine such a thing happening to Esther.

Jack came over to them. "Look, between us we still have one car left. Maybe you two could drive around and see if you see anything. I'll wait here by the phone."

"The police are already—" Esther began.

Mary said, "Oh, Esther, would you mind? I'll go crazy." She had already started to go crazy. Esther should understand that.

"If they're around here, someplace," Esther said. "But they might be heading toward New York."

"That'd be too risky," Jack pointed out. "If the police have put out a bulletin, they could be watching all the bridges and tunnels."

"She might not think of that," said Esther.

Mary said, "She thinks of everything. But they could

be just about anywhere. I slept for five hours. They could be in Pennsylvania."

She changed her shoes and met Esther at the car. As they drove out toward the highway, Esther asked, "Where do you want to try first?"

"I have no idea. She didn't even know the area. She always stuck around here, on the beach."

"Montauk way or the other way? Probably the other, okay? It'd be easier to get lost in the crowd."

"Esther, I just thought of something. Oh, God, why didn't I—She took her surfboard!"

22

"WHAT ARE YOU doing that for?" asked Fern.

Cinni, her hands black with mud, surveyed the mess she had made of the license plate.

"Covering up the number, so they can't read it. You don't want them to find us, do you?"

"I—don't know."

Jason asked, "When can we go home?"

Cinni's face dimpled with laughter. "What do you want to go home for?"

"I want to see my mommy."

"No, you don't, Jason. I'm your mommy now. We're going to my island. See, I brought my surfboard. As soon as it gets dark—"

"I want my real mommy."

There was a catch in his voice. He squeezed his eyes shut.

Cinni inched forward on her knees.

"Jason, you're going to stop that now. I said no noise." Her hand reached out and seized him in a tight grip. He stared in horror at the awful smelly mess of black swamp ooze on his arm. He took a breath to cry again, but managed to stop it.

"No noise," she repeated softly.

"Maybe he's hungry," Fern suggested.

"Then eat the rest of the bread." Cinni released his

arm and turned away, uninterested. She found a clean part of the bog, probably where a spring came up, and washed the mud from her hands.

"Back in the car now." She herded them ahead of her and locked them into the rear seat. Pretty cute of Gavin to have locks installed that could only be opened from the front. So his precious children couldn't *fall* out. That was a laugh.

"Where are we going now?" asked Fern.

"Don't ask questions. We've been here long enough. What's the matter, aren't you having fun?"

"No."

"You did at first. You thought it was funny to play a trick on Mommy."

Fern did not answer. It wasn't fun any more. She was afraid of Cinni. In the morning, on the familiar beach where they went every day, it had sounded adventurous to take a little ride, but she had assumed it would only be for a while. Now Cinni talked as if they were never going home. Just to think about it was like standing on the edge of emptiness. You *couldn't* think about it.

Even if they went to the island . . . Fern had stopped believing in the island. It was not a magic place where Cinni reigned as queen, it was only an island in the middle of the water, and they would have no house when it rained, no food except the loaf of bread they had taken from home, and that was almost gone, and no clothes but their bathing suits. And she was already feeling cold, since the sunshine had disappeared.

Worst of all, there would be no way back. Neither she nor Jason could swim. What if Cinni went away and left them there?

She glanced at Jason. He sat staring dumbly ahead, his mouth slightly open. He was too little to think of what could happen. Fern huddled in her corner of the seat and wished they were back home on the beach with their mother, back where they had left her this morning. She closed her eyes and wished—

The car lurched under her, and she smelled the sour swamp, which still clung to Cinni, and now to Jason. She couldn't wish it away. It was not a dream.

23

THE TRAIN WAS making every stop. Driving him up the wall. The longer it took, the more Gavin wondered what he was doing on it, anyway.

A commuter train to Mattapogue, hell. Who'd commute way out to Mattapogue? You'd have to be crazy.

He *was* crazy. That was the answer. Crazier even than his wife. She was the one who had hired the girl, but she hadn't known. At first he thought she must have seen it. Then he realized it was the kind of secret signal that comes across to a man. Not only was Mary a woman, but when you came right down to it, a rather naive one at that.

He had gotten the signal. It was, after all, intended for him. He had been appalled—only fourteen?—but he had also, he was forced to admit, been intrigued. You wouldn't ever guess it from her outward appearance. That made it all the more interesting.

And then—this. Hell and damn. He ought to have discussed it with Mary on Sunday, really cleared the air, so he wouldn't have done what she did. In fact, if he had followed her suggestion and taken the girl back with him . . . But it had seemed so precipitate at the time. And Martina was there. And the girl would have told.

So who'd have believed her?

Anybody might. He'd have betrayed himself somehow. And it would all be talked about, and who needed that?

What if she'd already said something? He didn't even want to be there. He wanted to stay in New York and pretend none of it happened.

But there were the children.

She wouldn't really hurt them. She wasn't that kind, in spite of Mary's hysteria. Mary tended to forget that Cinni was only a kid herself. Besides, the police were on it. What good could he do?

They stopped at another station. Probably about the fiftieth. He stared dully out at the weathered platform. He was diverted by the arrival of another train, going the other direction. Back to New York.

His chance. Probably his only chance. Oh, Jesus, he could just go back and she'd never know he had even started out. He wouldn't have to face them all, with that stupid girl blabbering. He could—go to California, even. Or Mexico.

The kids?

He would see them on the weekend. He would call as soon as he got home, to be sure they were all right.

He grabbed his jacket from the shelf above him, and dashed for the door.

The beach colony of Amagansett looked almost the same as their own. Mary wondered if Cinni would have had the gall to hide herself in one of those roads. They were all private, and it was close to Mattapogue, but then, Cinni specialized in gall.

"Esther, do you think—"

"What?" said Esther, slowing the car.

"Never mind. It was just an idea. This is very good of you," Mary added.

"I'd certainly want to be doing something if it were my kids," Esther replied. "In fact, this is good for me, too. I'm feeling with you. And who knows? You'd recognize that car faster than the police would."

It was true. She would. But there was practically no hope that the car would still be in the area.

"Where would she *go?* She's such an odd girl. I thought I knew her."

"Did she ever talk about any place? Some town she knew? People?"

"No, she'd never been out here before. And she wouldn't go home. I could find her there. But where else would she go?"

"No boyfriend?"

"She had a boyfriend, but he lived in the city, I think. And she was off of him. Wait a minute. Esther, she talked about a point. It was a place they discovered, on the Sound."

"Which Sound?"

"What do you mean?"

"Long Island Sound? Block Island? Besides, there are a million bays, and it's hard to know where the bays end and Block Island Sound begins."

"I can't remember. Maybe she didn't say. I just assumed it was Block Island Sound."

"That could be anywhere along there. She didn't happen to say anything else?"

"No. Only that it was beautiful and deserted."

"It gives us a starting place, anyway. *If* they went there." Again Esther slowed the car, and at the first opportunity, backed into a driveway and turned around.

"Where are we going?" Mary asked.

"We're going to start at Montauk."

"It wouldn't be Montauk. That's hardly deserted."

"Skip it, then?"

"No, I guess we'd better try everything. There's always a chance. I just don't know." Once again, Mary felt overcome with despair. This was silly, driving around like this. Looking for what amounted to a needle in a haystack. Or perhaps it was even more hopeless than that.

"We'd better find a phone," Esther said, "and call Jack. Maybe he's heard something."

Mary nodded. She would call the police, too, and tell them about the point. And they would know no more than they already did, because Long Island had several hundred miles of seashore, and by the time it was all searched, the children could be in Canada, or Florida. Or drowned.

"Esther, in a couple of hours it'll be dark."

"Maybe sooner," said Esther. "Look how cloudy it is."

Fern looked up at the sky. "Cinni, it's going to rain."

"Are you afraid of a little rain?" Cinni asked scornfully.

"No, but Jason's afraid of thunder."

"Jason's not going to be afraid with me, are you, sweetie?" Cinni turned around to smile at him, which made her swerve into the left lane. A car blew its horn furiously.

There was something about her smile that Jason no longer liked. He shook his head, because it was expected of him, but he was terribly afraid. There were goosebumps all over his skin. He shivered, with only his red plaid swimming trunks to keep him warm.

He snuggled next to Fern. Ordinarily, if they got near each other, they would begin punching and hitting, but now he needed her. And she did not push him away.

"I want to go home," he confided.

"So do I," she whispered.

He had hoped she would know what to do. But she was as helpless as he. It was terrifying.

"I don't want to go to the island," he said.

Neither of them wanted to go. They were cold and hungry and wanted their mother, and the island did not seem nearly as appealing as it once had. But none of that mattered to Cinni. And she had the power to do with them as she pleased.

They drove around Montauk Park, but from the road, they could see very little of the shore.

"You were right," said Esther. "They probably ouldn't be here, right under the noses of the Coast uard. I just thought she might try to hide in the owd, especially if she's too inexperienced to drive ry far.

They entered the parking lot and cruised through it, arching for the car.

"Did she take any clothes?" asked Esther.

"Not that I know of. I don't know what she owns. ow stupid of me to look for sleeping pills when I ould have been checking the children's clothes."

"She took her surfboard," Esther reminded her.

Mary made a sound in her throat, but no words came ut. She did not want to give it the reality of words, en in her mind. But there it was, with all that it im- lied: What if Cinni had taken clothes for herself, and ot for the children?

They parked the car and crossed the road to a restau- nt which had a back terrace overlooking the water.

"Here's your Block Island Sound," said Esther, "and ur ocean. Nuts, you can't see much of the shore from ere. I hoped we could find her damned point."

"Let's go on." They were wasting time.

Esther said, "I'd give my eye teeth for a pair of binoc- lars. Do you think we should go home and get binocu- rs?"

Mary shook her head. "It's going to be dark."

Besides, there was nothing to see.

"Where are we going now?" Fern asked as Cinni urned onto a narrower road that forked off from the ain highway.

"We're going here. And stop asking questions."

Fern watched carefully. This was not the place they ad discovered with Pete. This road was wider and—dif- erent. She saw rows of cars in a parking lot, and people verywhere, and some tents, and just beyond them, a each. She wished Cinni would turn in to the parking lot. Maybe she could run up to one of the people and ask for help.

But Cinni kept on going. The road wound over hills, past big houses with big cars in their driveways. Some of the houses were down over the hillside, and some were almost lost among the trees.

She would rather have gone to the point. At least she knew it. What were they doing here?

She wanted to ask, but Cinni was in a bad mood. She supposed it didn't matter what they were doing. They would have to do what Cinni told them, anyway.

"Are you ever going to take us home?" The question burst out before she could stop it.

"What do you want to go home for?" Cinni was not as angry as she had expected.

"I want my mommy and daddy."

"Oh, shut up with your mommy and daddy."

Fern slid onto the floor and curled into a ball, feeling soggy and weak with despair. A tear rolled down her cheek. Jason, who was getting onto the floor beside her, saw it, and he began to cry, too.

The car came to a stop. Fern raised her head. How strange. They were in back of a house. It was a large, yellowish house built on a hill, with the front part higher than the back part. Stone steps led down through a rock garden to the driveway, where they had parked. Cinni had brought the car right up against a pair of closed garage doors. Fern could not see the road from where they were. Only trees, and the house. She turned to look out of the back window. There was a path leading through some bushes toward the ocean.

Cinni did not move to get out of the car. No one came out of the house. It seemed very quiet and closed up. Gradually it dawned on Fern that there was no one in the house to come out of it.

"Why are we here?"

"We're going to wait till it gets dark," Cinni replied.

"Why?"

"So nobody will see us, stupid."

"And then what are we going to do?"

"Then we're going to my island."

"On a boat?"

"We don't have a boat, stupid. On my surfboard."

24
❧

MARY HAD SEEN only a fragment of the shore, but it was enough to remind her how big the world was.

"Esther, we're never going to find them," she said as they got back into the car. She could not remember how many times she had already said it, or thought it.

Esther gave her a quick look. "I should think she could very well get tired of the whole thing and bring them back. After all, what's she going to do with herself? She'll have to go home sometime. It's not like a real kidnapping, when you don't even know who the kidnapper is."

Mary leaned against the headrest and put her hands over her face. Would Cinni come slinking back with the children? Not likely.

"No," she said, "Cinni will think of something."

"She can't think of much, after she even called you and admitted she took the kids."

"But she had to do that. Otherwise I wouldn't know what I'm being punished for."

"You couldn't guess?"

"It's not what you'd think. It's more because I have Gavin." Did she have Gavin? "Anyhow, she probably wanted to hear my voice. You know. Hear how I was taking it."

Cinni had not given her a chance to speak, but the

contact was there all the same. That, alone, might have been satisfying.

"Shall we go down the Old Montauk Highway?" Esther asked. "We didn't go that way. It runs closer to the shore, on the ocean side. There are some fancy houses, and a campground."

Mary looked around hopefully as Esther took a fork from the main highway, but her hope soon disappeared. This was too settled an area.

"Not much place to hide around here, is there?" she said.

"I'm afraid not," Esther agreed sadly. "Every time I see a little road going off, it turns out to be a driveway."

Ordinarily, Mary would have enjoyed such a trip, intrigued as she was by houses. She could not tell much about the interiors, but the houses themselves were set in pockets among the trees and on the hillside that sloped down toward the ocean. There was a particularly lovely one below the road level, a yellow stucco in a manicured clearing, with a very steep driveway that looped around to the back of the house, and its own private access to the beach. It did not look inhabited.

"Well, I'm sorry, hon," Esther said as they passed the campground. "I just thought maybe. I forgot it was so built up."

Mary twisted to see into the parking lot. Esther offered to drive the car in.

"No, they wouldn't be there," Mary decided. "It's too public. I even see a police car. Esther, isn't it odd? She never told me not to call the police. Either she didn't think of it, or she was so damn sure of herself that she figured it wouldn't make any difference."

And maybe she was right.

Jack Reardon found himself pacing back and forth near the telephone, as Mary said she had done. It was all this damn waiting that got to a person. He could have been the one to drive the car, but he had thought that

Esther might be more soothing for Mary. At least Mary knew her better.

When the telephone rang, he whirled around and stared at it for a moment. He was almost afraid he had imagined its ringing, just because he wanted something to happen.

An angry voice demanded, "Who is this?"

"Is that Gavin? Jack Reardon here."

"Oh. Sorry. Where's Mary?"

Jack explained where Mary was. Gavin took that, correctly, to mean that nothing more had been heard about the children. "Is Mary okay?" he asked.

"Not really," Jack replied. "That's why I suggested she go out with Esther. It didn't seem too likely they could find anything, but it helps, you know?"

"Not a word from the girl?" Gavin sounded as if he could hardly believe it.

"Not since she phoned to say she had the kids. Where are you calling from?"

"Railroad station. Mattapogue." Now he sounded sheepish.

"Wait there till Esther phones in. I'll have her go and pick you up."

Ten minutes later Jack stood at the screen door, smoking his pipe and watching a pair of headlights come down the road. They slowed to a stop in front of the house. He was about to go out and tell Esther to turn around, when he saw that it was a taxi, and Gavin was getting out of it.

He must have come straight from the office. His shirt was open, his tie was in his pocket, and he carried an attaché case.

He hadn't known about Cinni's phone call.

"After you told me, I thought I'd better come straight over," he said in something like a mumble. "Maybe she'll call again. It still seems crazy. I can't believe it. I almost got off the damn train."

"Mary'll be glad you're here."

"Maybe."

They were silent. Now it was Gavin who paced. Jack could not bring himself to sit down, but hovered edgily by the telephone, knocking his pipe against his teeth.

Finally Gavin seemed to recollect that he was the host. "Care for a beer?" He went to the kitchen and brought back two. He drank his all at once, then crumpled the can in his fist.

"She never should have hired that girl."

"She didn't know," said Jack.

Gavin did not respond, so Jack went on. "We've had some lulus in our day, but I have to admit, nothing like this. There's no way you can tell just from an interview. Still, most people, you know, they're honest and sincere. And a girl for the summer—a perfectly nice high school girl—you'd never imagine."

Gavin grunted an answer. He went to the front door and stared out at the gathering darkness.

He had known. A whole week ago, he had known what she was like. At least sexually. He hadn't dreamed she'd take the kids, or anything like that. Maybe he ought to have realized her sexual precocity was a bad sign. The way she wanted to sneak behind Mary's back. Her interest in him, the children's father.

It just seemed easier not to realize such things. To hope it would all work out. And then he'd gotten himself trapped.

Anyhow, nothing could beat hindsight. It *might* have worked out.

A car was coming down the road. When it passed the Reardons' house he began to hope, and dread at the same time, that it would be Cinni with the kids.

It was the Reardons' car. He was still standing in the lighted doorway where Mary could see him. She must have seen him, but she gave no sign until she reached the door and simply said, "Oh. Gavin."

He held the door open. Both women walked past him. Esther asked, "When did you get here?"

"A little while ago," he said. "No word yet."

Esther described where they had searched. Jack picked up the phone and called the police for a report. Nothing.

"We're here to hold a war council," Esther told the men. "There's a particular place where Mary thinks she just might be, but we don't know where that place is."

"Or maybe she wouldn't be there," Mary said. "She might remember that she told me about it."

"Did you tell the police?" Gavin asked. She nodded. Her eyes avoided his. He wondered how much she knew.

He sidled over to her, put his arm around her and patted her shoulder. She did not resist.

Esther opened a map of Long Island and spread it on the dining table.

"It's hard to tell from this where there are any small deserted points," she said. "And there are always those insignificant dirt roads that don't show on the map."

Mary said, "When they talked about it, they mentioned seeing some islands."

"You can see islands from anywhere along that shore," Jack reminded her.

"Fern said 'the island.' Or *an* island. She emphasized it."

"Maybe Gardiner's Island. That's pretty big and noticeable. But it doesn't tell us much. We don't know from what angle they were seeing the island, or whether it even was Gardiner's."

"But it was a deserted point," said Esther. "At least that's how Mary says they described it. We ought to be able to narrow it down somehow."

Mary looked out of the window. "It's dark now. We can't find them in the dark. I don't know why I thought they'd go to that point, necessarily. They could be anywhere on Long Island, or off it. It's been such a long time."

Again Gavin patted her shoulder, but it was really a futile gesture.

25

FERN SAID, "IT'S dark, Cinni. Why aren't we going anywhere?"

Cinni, in the front seat, turned partway around. "What's your hurry?"

Fern was not in any hurry at all. She only wanted to know.

"Let's stay here," she answered quickly.

"Don't you want to go to my island? You wanted to before."

"You scared me today."

"Me, too," said Jason.

"I scared you? How?" Now Cinni turned all the way, but it was dark, and Fern could see her face only dimly.

"The way you acted," Fern said reluctantly. "You were mean to us."

"Like your mommy was mean this morning?"

Cinni had her there. Mommy certainly had been mean, screaming and yanking them around by the arm. It was all, Cinni had explained, because Mommy didn't like Cinni. And Mommy didn't like her because Daddy and Fern and Jason liked her. Mommy was jealous; she wanted them all to herself.

And selfish, Fern had thought at the time. Why shouldn't they like Cinni? Even Mommy used to like

Cinni, but Mommy was a little bit crazy, according to Cinni, because she had a baby in her tummy.

Still, never to see Mommy again? It was impossible. Certainly she was not always crazy and mean. She usually took them to interesting places, and they had fun together.

"We never went to the ice-cream store," Fern said. "She promised we could go there."

"Shut up with the ice-cream store."

"Is there ice cream on your island?"

"Gallons," said Cinni. She sounded tired. If she was tired, how would they get there?

"Cinni, I don't want to go on your surfboard. I don't like the water at night. It's black and scary."

"I'm cold," said Jason.

"You guys are fussing an awful lot," Cinni remarked in a soft, buttery voice. "I don't like fussy kids."

Fern felt brave enough to suggest, "Maybe if you take us home, we wouldn't fuss."

"You don't want to go home to a mean mommy."

"She's not mean." Again that hopeless feeling. "I like her. She's my mommy."

"Don't you like me?"

Fern started to answer, but did not exactly know how to explain. "You're not my mommy," she said.

"I am now."

"No, you're not!"

Cinni switched on the engine and made it roar. Fern put her hands to her ears. She had never heard it roar like that. Maybe it was going to blow up.

The car lurched backward and jerked to a violent stop. Then it shot backward again. Fern screamed.

Damn hell.

Now the car was wrecked. She had done something wrong and it went into reverse instead of forward. At least it didn't go far. It had crashed into the trees before it could land in the ocean, but she didn't think she would be able to get it out, or drive it again.

At least she was in one piece. Unhurt. She heard the children crying. Why not just leave them there? But, shit, that would not be enough. They'd get found, and the only one to be permanently affected by this whole thing would be Cinni, and that wasn't fair.

But now she couldn't drive over to that point, where she planned to take them out to a deserted island and bury them. That way, it would be years before they were ever found, and that would serve the parents right, those goddam bitches. That Gavin, chickening out, afraid she would have him arrested for screwing her. Well, screw him, she had no such intention. She only wanted to get pregnant so he would marry her.

He refused to give her a child, so she had taken his. She had great plans for them.

It would have worked, too. All of it. She had her clothes in a watertight plastic bag, and all of Mary's money pinned inside her bra. She would go on to the mainland, hitch a ride somewhere, get a job, and start living.

But now, damn; they were on the ocean side, and there were no islands, and what was she to do?

"Damn you kids, stop that noise, you're not hurt."

"I wanna go *home*," wept Fern.

"Me, too," bawled Jason. "I'm cold."

His teeth were chattering, she could hear it. Dumb brat. It was all their parents' fault. If they had been nice to her, the kids wouldn't have to die.

But they had not been nice.

"Oh, shit, I guess we'll have to go from here."

The door was jammed. She had to kick it, but finally she got it open. Then she hauled the kids out, and her surfboard.

She was angry. This was not the way she had planned it. She would have to take them out deep and drown them, but their bodies would wash ashore, and then the parents would know. She would have preferred that they did not know for a long, long time. It would keep them bleeding.

If she had some kind of weight . . . Damn it to hell, they'd find the car anyway, and know where to look. Damn her stupid mistake.

It was Pete's fault. He should have let her practice driving the van.

"Come on, kids, down to the water. It's island time."

Damn the wind. It might knock them off the surfboard before she was out far enough to sink them properly. But she supposed it wouldn't really matter, as long as they were sunk one way or another.

Then she could swim ashore and hitchhike, as she'd originally planned. Who would think anything of a teenager with wet hair, hitchhiking near the beach in summer? They'd be looking for a girl with two small children.

Look again, you bitches. The laugh is on you.

26

MARY AND GAVIN waited in the car while Jack went to get something from his house. They would keep it up all night, probably, this useless search, just for the sake of being busy. Esther was the one to stay by the telephone this time.

Gavin reached out and put his hand over Mary's. Something in her brain told her to respond, but she could not. She was numb.

They were his children, too, said her brain.

Still she could not move.

Jack came around the car, a gray and green box tucked under his arm, and got in behind the wheel. He handed the box to Mary.

"That's a walkie-talkie set," he explained. "It belongs to my kids. Sometimes they can pick up police calls on it. I just thought it might help a little, keep us in touch."

She did not see how a walkie-talkie set could help find the children. She did not know of anything that could help.

She felt suddenly stifled. She was squeezed between the two men, and wished she were alone in the back seat where she could cry or simply explode, but Jack had already started the car. At least she could see better from the front. That was more important.

Gavin held the map on his knee. She wished she had never mentioned the point. Now everyone was in a rut about it. And there was no reason to believe Cinni would go there. More likely she would take the children as far away as she could, and their only hope lay in some gas-station attendant's recognizing the car from a police bulletin.

She knew Cinni was well fixed to buy gas. Not only had she emptied all the cash from Mary's purse, but she had taken the car registration and credit cards as well.

Gavin asked, "How long were they gone that day they found the point?"

"I don't know. Two or three hours. But they bought the surfboard in that time, and they bought ice cream, and I don't know what else they did. Maybe they stopped for lunch. Gavin, I don't think we should concentrate too much on that point."

"We have to concentrate on something. It makes a place to start."

The walkie-talkie crackled and sputtered. She could hear voices, but they spoke in some Martian language, backward and accelerated. It jarred her, distracting her attention from the dark, empty road.

"It's not saying anything."

"I've got the antenna all the way up," Gavin replied. "We're in a bad receiving area, that's all."

"Those are taxi calls," said Jack.

"How can you tell?"

"That's the other thing they can get on that gadget. They get it more often than police calls."

She did not want to listen to taxi calls.

"Do you think—She wouldn't really hurt them, would she?"

Again Gavin put his hand over hers. She was mildly surprised at how big and warm it felt.

But he did not answer her question.

"Come on, get moving."

"I can't see," wept Fern.

"Do as I say, or you're dead. Remember the jellyfish?"

This was not Cinni. This was a monster. Fern began to

walk cautiously, then her foot skidded out from under her and she fell down.

"It's slippery!" she wailed.

"Get up and move. And hurry."

"I can't."

"That's just pine needles. Now move."

Fern wanted to hold Cinni's hand for guidance. At the same time, she did not want to touch her. She wondered what would happen if she were to run away and hide among the bushes. Cinni might not be able to find her in the dark.

She looked up at the sky. It was black and boiling, with a spot of bright cloud. Then the brightness disappeared. It was the moon. And if the clouds opened again, then Cinni could find her in the moonlight.

They left the mat of pine needles and walked across rough, hard stones that hurt her feet. And she was cold. Cinni wore a sweatshirt over her bathing suit, but Fern and Jason had nothing.

The moon came out again. It was only part of a moon, not very bright. But where would she go if she got away? And what if Cinni caught her? And what would happen to Jason? She kept on walking, stumbling in the dark.

27

❦

"TURN THAT THING off, please?" Mary begged. The screeches and squawks coming over the walkie-talkie were driving her mad.

Gavin was about to protest, but Jack said, "Yeah, turn it off. It's no good right now, we're in a bad area."

Mary had no idea what area they were in. It seemed almost dreamlike, this endless pursuit in the dark, except for the reality that was there like a headache, pounding at her.

From time to time she would open a curtain in her mind and try to see her life as it might be without the children. She would quickly close it again. She could not face it. She wondered if she could ever face it. And yet it happened sometimes to other people. How did they manage?

Would she ever have to be one of those other people?

She had been watching out of the window with part of her mind alert—certainly she would have known if she saw anything—but part of her was in a dull trance. It surprised her when Jack stopped the car. They were outside a tavern of some kind. The sounds of voices and occasional laughter came from within.

"I'll give Esther a call," said Jack, as he got out of the car.

In her trancelike state, Mary had forgotten Gavin

eside her. He put his arm around her and drew her
ose to him.

"I guess it's pretty stupid to say I'm sorry," he
umbled. "That doesn't help the kids. Or you."

"You should have taken her back," Mary replied
ully.

"Not that. I'm sorry for a lot of things. God, I almost
ot off the train."

She heard the words and vaguely wondered what train
e almost got off of. Nothing made sense. They were
asting time, sitting there.

"I forgot—was such an idiot," he explained, without
xplaining.

*I want to get back on the road, dammit, why is Jack
king so long?*

"—was acting like a high school kid. There are some
ings you have to put behind you. I was irresponsible.
orgot how young—impressionable—I think she really
1ought—Never mind."

"It's all right, Gavin." Her hand crept out and found
is, the one he didn't have around her shoulders. It
adn't been all right. Perhaps it was now. She glanced at
im, and in the dim light, saw his anguish—the strained
1outh, his eyes, as though in pain, staring ahead through
1e windshield. And if they never saw the children
gain, that look would go on forever.

Never saw the children?

He shook his head. He meant it was not all right, not
eally. She supposed, in a way, she had brought it on
erself.

"You know me," she said. "I was living in a dream
·orld."

He gave her hand a brief squeeze. It had always been a
·ke between them, the dream world she lived in. But it
·asn't funny.

"No, I mean it. I was childish, too. I wanted every-
1ing perfect in my little dream world, and perfect
1eant taking Fern and Jason to the park—" Her voice

broke. "—and reading poetry with them. I forgot about you. That was irresponsible, too."

She wept against his shoulder. He pulled a handkerchief from his pocket. He always carried a clean handkerchief.

"I can't make excuses," he said, wiping the tears from her face. "There is no excuse."

What is Jack doing?

When Mary had calmed herself, she went on talking. It was better to talk.

"There was a hunger in her. I should have seen it. A hunger, I think, for—what I had. But I didn't want to see it. I didn't believe it."

"I saw part of it. I could have helped, and I didn't. And now, if anything happens—"

Jack came out of the tavern. "Jesus," he said. "Only one phone in that place. Esther was fairly busting. The police found a car that might be yours."

Mary's hand flew to her mouth to stifle a cry. Of hope. Despair. *How* had they found the car? Empty?

Gavin jerked his arm away from her and turned on the walkie-talkie, adjusted the antenna, held the speaker to his ear.

"That's all I could get," said Jack. "It was somewhere on the Old Montauk Highway."

"Only the car?" Mary asked in a tight voice.

"Only the car. They're searching the area. They're bringing in some dogs, but it will take a while."

But we were there. On the Old Montauk Highway.

"Oh, please," she whispered.

Jack said, "I can't go any faster, Mary."

Trees obscured the road above, but through them Cinni could see flashing lights. God damn. Oh, well, it was kind of funny that it took them so long. And maybe they wouldn't think of looking out in the water.

Fern made a sound as if to speak, and Cinni clapped a hand over her mouth.

"Not one peep out of you kids, understand?" she mut-red through clenched teeth. "Not one damn bit of oise, or in you go."

Damn that wind. It was hard to paddle against it. All he had to paddle with was her legs from the knee down, nd her hands, because the only way they could all fit on he board was to sit upright. It was really too wide for ason's legs. After she dumped the kids, she could lie own and move much faster, but she would have to be retty damn far out, because they would make a noise, robably, and sounds carry like crazy over water.

She tried to figure how she could do it. Maybe rangle Fern without Jason knowing, since he was in the ront, and then strangle him.

She was glad she had remembered the sweatshirt. At ast she wouldn't have to use up energy just keeping varm. The children were shivering, but she couldn't elp that. It had never occurred to her to bring sweaters or them.

A wave washed over the surfboard, making it lurch. 'ern gurgled in fear, and Jason began to whimper softly. Iell, now the edge of her sweatshirt was wet.

Again she whispered, "Shut up, you goddam brats."

Fern responded with a muffled sob. The shirt felt asty. She removed her hands from the water long nough to turn up the wet part so that it did not touch er skin.

Shit, they scarcely seemed to be moving. Those damn rats were just too heavy. She began to paddle harder. The important thing was to get rid of them as fast and as afely as possible.

It was easier than they had expected to find the right lace. They saw flashing lights through the trees. Mary elt a moment of astonished recognition. It was the yel-ow stucco house she had admired.

What if they were there when she and Esther drove ast? Oh, God, what if they had been there all the time?

Jack nosed the car down the steep driveway.

Gavin said, "I hope they're not going to concentrate it all in one place, just because of the car."

"How far do you think they can get on foot?" asked Jack.

Mary said, "We went right by here, Esther and I."

Two police cars stood in the turning space at the end of the driveway. A policeman tried to wave Jack away.

"It's the parents," Jack shouted. To Mary and Gavin, he said, "You get out here. I'll park somewhere."

They climbed out, Gavin holding her hand. She was blinded for a moment by the lights. Gavin drew her away, over to the bushes, where she recognized it. Their station wagon. It was backed in at a wild angle and the side-view mirror was smashed.

"The number checks," a policeman told them. "We cleaned off the license plates. There was mud all over them. Deliberate, it looked like."

"She didn't miss a trick, did she?" said Gavin.

The car was empty. A front and a back door stood open, and the tailgate was down.

"That's the way we found it," the policeman explained. "We've got people searching the woods and the shore area."

"Her surfboard!"

Mary started running down a narrow path toward the water. She slipped on pine needles, grasped at a tree branch to catch herself.

Maybe Cinni had left the children on shore. But the police would have found them. Oh, God.

Away from the lights, the path was dark. She tripped on a stone and pitched forward, wrenching her ankle.

Gavin caught up with her. He tried to hold her arm. "Easy, Mary. The police are looking."

She slapped him away. *"Don't you see? She opened the tailgate to get out her surfboard!"*

"Surfboard? She wouldn't—" But he ran along with her. His feet were sure. In sneakers. He must have changed at the house. Gavin thought of everything.

Then they were wading through beach sand. Flashlights dotted the shore, glinting on uniforms and white sports shirts. A man with a notebook tried to ask them questions. "Go to hell," said Gavin, pushing past him. A light exploded in their faces. Gavin swore again, calling the photographer a goddam vulture.

Again blinded, Mary stumbled toward one of the policemen. "Did you find a surfboard?"

"Surfboard?"

"She took her surfboard."

All around her there was noise, lights, the gabble and static of a walkie-talkie. Then another flashbulb. "Leave us alone, can't you?" she begged.

The policeman looked out toward the water. It was too dark to see anything.

"I don't think she'd take it out," said Gavin. "This is open ocean. It's rough, Mary."

"You didn't think she'd do a lot of things she did."

The policeman said, "She could have picked up another car.

Maybe Pete. Maybe she called Pete. Maybe she stole another car.

With the lights on shore, and the reflections, it was impossible to see any distance out into the water. She looked up at the sky, at the rolling dark clouds. One spot began to glow, where the moon was. She shaded her eyes and tried again to see the water. Black emptiness. They wouldn't be there. It was too rough.

"No, wait. There! There!"

It was gone. A mirage. She wanted it so badly that she had created it.

"I thought—"

The policeman raised a pair of binoculars.

Only a mirage. A thought form. It had seemed almost real.

"Wait a second," he said.

Gavin took off his shoes and stepped out into the surf, away from the lights.

The policeman stared. "There *is* something out there!"

"Where?" She snatched the binoculars. She could see nothing. Her whole body went into a fit of trembling.

"I can't—"

"Jesus, if it's them, they'll get swamped," said the officer. He tried to take back his binoculars. She held them tightly. For just a moment she thought she saw—

The glasses were wrenched from her hand. People shouted all around her. She felt like jelly.

Gavin said, "They're out there? You saw them?" Nobody knew for sure. "You got a bullhorn? Maybe if we tell her—"

"No, Gavin!" She clutched at his arm. "She'll know we've seen her. She'll do something—"

A voice in back of her called to someone on the path. "Tell them to bring a searchlight and a boat."

She was horrified. She thought the police had everything ready. "How long will it take to get a boat?"

No one paid attention to her. The man with the binoculars exclaimed, "I see them. I've got 'em now. Hell, it's rough out there."

"How long will it take to get a boat?"

"Too long," he said.

She could see them now, shadows against the lighter sky. Saw them struggling against the wind and the waves, three figures like steps, the smallest one in front.

My Jason. That's my Jason. Only a baby.

She was barely aware that she kicked off her sandals and plunged into the water. She did not feel the cold or see the darkness.

Gavin called after her, "Wait, Mary, the baby!"

There were other shouts. She did not, at the moment, know what baby he was talking about. She swam toward where she had seen them.

Her dress dragged at her knees. There was a heaviness in her belly—yes, the baby—but she could manage.

They were hidden again. She could only guess where they were, and swam as straight as she could. She dared not take even a moment to look back and get a fix from the shore.

Please, God, let them hang on.

The water churned around her. She had to fight against the waves. How could they sit on a surfboard and not be washed away?

I'm coming, I'm coming. They could not swim. Once they fell off, they would drown. She did not think about Cinni at all.

The water began to brighten. A faint silvery cast spread over it. Against the silver, she could see a dark and white shape.

It was not the same shape as before. No more steps, but a tangle. She thought she heard faint cries.

"I'm coming!" She could not make a sound. The strain was telling on her. *He's right, I'll lose the baby. I can feel it. Too tired. . . .*

She could barely move her arms. Couldn't see them. Everything gone. *I'll die.*

Then another silver frost on the water. A very pale one. She saw the dark struggling tangle, the gleam of the surfboard. But how many were still there?

Oh, God, let them be safe. It isn't fair. My children. . . .

She would never reach them. A heart attack. Her heart was dying.

Stop it, she told herself. *Stop thinking.*

Suddenly she could see them clearly. Cinni's face, Cinni's arms, clinging to the surfboard and battling something. Jason! Beating his hands and pushing him away.

A low, steady cry. Fern, apart from the others, gasping, pumping savagely to stay afloat.

Mary forced a voice from her exhausted body. "Fern— Tread easy—Get Jason."

Fern shrieked, "Mommy!" The last of it was swallowed in water.

From somewhere in back of her, she heard Gavin. "I'll get her. You go for Jason."

Was it really Gavin? She had thought she was alone.

Jason—She reached out. He was gone. Little Jason. She tried to move. Her limbs were useless.

Then the water broke and his head came up. A round shadow. Another mirage. And it vanished.

She remembered the exact place. Could she do it? Push herself under? Even in normal conditions, it took strength to dive from the surface.

She gathered what breath she could. Her face went into the water, but she could not propel her body downward.

Her hand touched something. It could have been anything. She grabbed.

As she pulled him to the surface, she knew that this, finally, was the last thing she could do. Jason gagged and tried to gulp in air. He was choking to death on water, and she could not move.

She lay back and floated, trying as best she could, with arms that had no more feeling, to hold him above the surface. It was all she could manage, while he choked to death.

Suddenly Gavin was beside her. A terrified Fern clung to his back, squeezing his neck so tightly that he could scarcely breathe. Mary saw his chin go under the water and his mouth open. He raised his arms to take Jason.

Mary tried to say "Float, Fern." The words became lost in splashing water, and another sound.

A droning sound. A hornet, she thought. A wasp, a bumblebee. Or a blender.

Jason would die. No one to help him. Four minutes and his brain would die.

She listened again for the blender, thinking dimly that it might be able to help, but she could not hear it any more.

From the bow of the boat that floated becalmed, a man watched the scene through a pair of binoculars, while his companion wrestled with the stalled engine.

"They've got the kids, but there's trouble. One of 'em's not moving. I can't see—"

"You'd better start rowing," said the man at the engine. He jerked the starter cord. The motor sputtered and died. It had been the nearest boat, but it was a very old one. He pulled again and again. A haze of exhaust surrounded the engine. He could smell it. And those people were dying.

"Aw, Christ," he exclaimed in frustration. A whole family out there dying. Just a little too far away.

Again Mary tried to aim her hands. She tried to reach Fern's arm. She could not tell whether she had touched anything, or whether or not she had even moved. Fern was too frightened to let go of her father.

Mary floated. She was in clouds now. A knife-sharp pain struck her abdomen and woke her briefly. She doubled over in agony without realizing it, and choked on water.

Gavin was hitting the baby. She moaned, to stop him. Gavin's face sank under the water. Going, gone.

The baby let out a cry. It was born? Right there?

Then the baby turned into Jason. She was losing her mind. She floated, floated, and thought of home. Had they locked the door? Turned out all the lights? This was so final. She wished she could go back and make sure the door was locked.

From far away, someone called her name. That proved she was dying. It was a man's voice. Her father. She could not see anything.

They took something from her hands. She reached for it, knowing it should not have been taken, although she had no idea what it was.

Then someone grasped her under the arms and lifted her. What an odd way to die. She was set down heavily. When she looked up, she saw the sky, with a half moon just beginning to appear from behind the clouds.

It was real. She tried to say it, but her lips failed to move.

Gradually her consciousness returned. She found Fern lying beside her and saw Gavin collapsed against the gunwale. A man in a yellow windbreaker held Jason over his knee and slapped his back.

"You did pretty well out there," the man said. "Got him breathing again, but he's still full of water."

She closed her eyes as Jason vomited water onto the floor of the boat.

Something bumped against the boat, and someone screamed.

"My surfboard! Get my *surfboard!*"

A man said, "Take it easy, sister. You've got your life. That's enough for now."

Mary opened her eyes. Cinni was huddled in the bow, looking small and shapelessly pale with her blond hair streaming into the wet mass of a white sweatshirt.

"I had to do it," Cinni explained to the men. "She went crazy, their mother." A disdainful jerk of her chin toward Mary. "She was hitting them and dragging them around by their little arms. I had to get them away."

"Better not make any statements," said the man in the yellow windbreaker.

Even now, thought Mary. She'll tell them everything, and that will invalidate the arrest, somehow.

She did not really know whether they arrested fourteen-year-olds. What did they do with fourteen-year-olds?

So young. And so clever.

Mary choked, and some of the water and salt cleared from her throat.

"Cinni? Out there on the water—why did you hit Jason and push him away? Were you trying to kill him?"

In the faint light, she could see Cinni's look of reproach and indignation.

"He was grabbing onto my *hair*. It hurt."

Gavin muttered, "So that's a capital offense, is it?" He edged closer to Mary. "I wonder how it feels to be the hub of the universe."

"I wonder if she can ever change," said Mary.

Inside her, the baby kicked with such force that her dress moved slightly.

Gavin placed his hand on her belly. "It's all right, kid. The worst is over."

His mouth against Mary's tasted of salt.